The Lotus Eaters

The Lotus Eaters

Marianne Macdonald

W F HOWES LTD

This large print edition published in 2007 by
W F Howes Ltd
Unit 4, Rearsby Business Park, Gaddesby Lane,
Rearsby, Leicester LE7 4YH

1 3 5 7 9 10 8 6 4 2

First published in the United Kingdom in 2006
by William Heinemann

A CIP catalogue record for this book is available
from the British Library

ISBN 978 1 40741 218 4

Typeset by Palimpsest Book Production Limited,
Grangemouth, Stirlingshire
Printed and bound in Great Britain
by Antony Rowe Ltd, Chippenham, Wilts.

For my parents

The charmed sunset linger'd low adown
In the red West: thro' mountain clefts the dale
Was seen far inland, and the yellow down
Border'd with palm, and many a winding vale
And meadow, set with slender galingale;
A land where all things always seem'd the same!
And round about the keel with faces pale,
Dark faces pale against that rosy flame,
The mild-eyed melancholy Lotos-eaters came.

From 'The Lotos-Eaters' (1832),
Alfred Lord Tennyson.

CHAPTER 1

I met Patty Belle at the Beverly Hills Hotel in September 1998. Clinton was in the depths of his disgrace, commentators were lamenting the moral bankruptcy of America and the Western world was in the midst of the biggest gold rush in history.

The great greedy boom rolled in the air. It was the peak of the Internet madness: a time of reckless extravagance, paper fortunes – the overthrow of an outdated era. It was a crazy time, a fantastic, never-to-be-repeated bubble, and whenever I think of it I think of Patty. She was just as seductive, and built on just as many illusions – but she had the same ecstasy of hope in her, too, that was dazzling.

I was still doing celebrity interviews. Commissioned by *The Times* to interview the singer Alanis Morissette in LA, knowing no one in Hollywood, I asked everyone I knew for people to call. I drew a blank until I bumped into an actor from my old college in Soho House – I hadn't seen him for years.

'I know someone,' he said, 'an actress. She'll fry your brain.'

He scribbled a name and a number on a match-book in keen, cramped longhand: Patty Bell. I frowned. 'Why will she fry my brain?'

He gave a nostalgic grin as a fly banged against the sash window. 'Call her and see.'

'But is she nice?' I demanded. He had jammed his phone into his back pocket, ready to leave: he gave a knowing chuckle, smoothing back his long blond hair with his palms.

'She just is,' he said. 'You like adventures. Call her and see.'

He left and I dropped the matchbook into the bottom of my bag and forgot about it: I had no intention of following it up.

But in LA, after four days alone, I changed my mind. I dialled the number. It buzzed a long time, no answer-phone. I was about to hang up when a voice fell breathlessly down the line, girlish, English, wary: 'Hello?'

'Oh, hi,' I said. 'I'm sorry to bother you,' and explained who I was. At which the voice changed.

'Oh, *hi*! I thought you were someone else. That's why I was being funny. First I wasn't going to get the phone, then I had to run, then I tripped on the stairs.' A giggle. 'Don't you always trip over on the stairs? I do, it's like some kind of a *curse*. But Jake: how is he? Wow, we had some fun' – which is how I came to meet Patty Bell, or Belle, as she liked to spell it, in one of those random encounters that change your life for good.

We had arranged to meet at noon by the Beverly

Hills Hotel pool: her suggestion. I went early to read the paper in the sun. It was quiet. A plump waiter in white shorts was spraying tables with cleaning fluid. Another was talking to his mother on the bartender's phone. The sun fell in a sheer hot blanket, drying out the brown rainwater glinting round the fallen green leaves, the pink bougainvillea, the blue and white sunbeds. Close up, I saw that the place had a faint air of decay: the chunky leather menus were stained, my glass tabletop chipped, even the bougainvillea plants were plastic – only the seething surface of the pool seemed absolutely clean.

The news was all about Clinton. That week he had testified to the grand jury about Monica Lewinsky. Unlike her, he had been unable to recall the details of their meetings in the White House corridors, the presents he had given, the endearments he had used. Now Starr had formally accused him of perjury, obstruction of justice and abuse of power. That morning, as the sun grilled my scalp, I read the latest piece on that tangled, sordid scandal, which would echo, in macrocosm, the affair with Patty. The moral abdication was just the same, his carelessness and self-absorption were hers . . .

It is not a good idea to make a charismatic sociopath the leader of one's party, or the President of one's country. Clinton is a superb campaigner, but there is a piece

3

missing. He has no moral compass; he does not know right from wrong. His is a sexual addiction. Women are 'bimbo eruptions'; the technique 'rub-a-dub'.

Rub-a-dub? I looked up, smiling. God, it was hot.

. . . because the psychological truth about Clinton is straightforward. He is not a madman; he does not hate humans; he is simply obsessed with power. He has been an associate of the Arkansas criminal and bond dealer Dan Lasater, convicted for distributing cocaine and later pardoned by Clinton. One of the first things Clinton did on assuming the Presidency was to appoint Patsy Thomasson – an aide of Lasater's – as director of the White House Office of Administration. Clinton also installed his close friend Webster Hubbell as Associate Attorney General, until Hubbell pleaded guilty to mail fraud and tax evasion charges connected with his handling of billing at the Rose Law Firm in Little Rock, which had partners that once included Hillary Clinton and Vince Foster . . .

The gate clanged. A woman came down the faded pink steps, humming in the white core of the sun. She set each foot down slowly, with a kind of pleasure, and her skin melted white like a candle. She had the figure of a Forties siren, crammed into a straining cream cotton dress. She radiated a kind of joyful, don't-care sensuality: you wanted to know her – you wanted to be her. Yet she gave off a strange sense of endurance, too, as if she might put up with things you couldn't even imagine . . .

I stood up. 'Are you Patty? I'm Lottie.'

'Oh, *hi*!' She grinned and ran down the last three steps towards me. 'I thought that must be you. Looking so cool and elegant.' Her gaze fell on my drink and her lips parted. 'Gosh: that looks amazing.'

'It's a Virgin Mary,' I said. 'Would you like one?'

But she pushed out her mouth. 'I don't know. It looks sort of bloody, and it's too early in the morning for blood. It's just the kind of morning you'd bump into a corpse; in fact, I just did: I followed a hearse right across Sunset. So you're Jake's girlfriend?' Unconsciously she brought her thumb to her mouth and chewed on it. She had a faint moustache, I saw, and her cheeks were a fraction too heavy for absolute beauty.

'God, no,' I said. 'No, I've not seen him for years. We were at Oxford together. I bumped into him in Soho the other day. He gave me your number.'

'What can I get you?' asked the plump waiter. He smiled at Patty.

'Definitely champagne,' she said. She shrugged. 'It gives you bad breath – but what the hell. I need

5

some. I tell you, when I get to be a star, which I probably won't, now I'm leaving, I'm going to drink champagne from morning till night.'

She widened her eyes and grinned, perhaps at the fantasy, perhaps at the treat to come, and the waiter grinned back, enchanted.

I smiled too. She was so joyful – so pretty, so unselfconscious, so eager. And, I thought, impossible to place. Her accent was flat, classless – with strange, precise consonants and an American softening to the end of her sentences. She was rummaging in her bag – for Marlboros, it turned out. She waved the packet at me.

'Thanks, I've given up.'

'Gosh; you're clever.' She poked the cigarette between her lips. 'I keep trying to. I have to, or I'll be a hag by forty. And you can't smoke anywhere in LA.' She lit up, as if in contradiction to this. 'The longest I did was a month. But then I met Ed and I got going again. How did you do it?'

'Give up? My father paid for me to do a detox in Switzerland.'

'Oh, wow. I guess you'd have to stop in Switzerland. It's so pure there, and everything.'

As if a thought had struck her, she looked away, picking at the skin round her thumb. I perceived she had some kind of trouble in her life. The skin round her nails was bitten and her hands, I saw, were the one flaw in her beauty: large-knuckled and criss-crossed by tiny red lines.

'You're all set,' said the waiter. He put down her

drink and retreated awkwardly, stiff with admiration. She didn't notice. 'Are you an actress too?'

'God, no. I do celebrity interviews.'

'You *do*?' She took a drag of her cigarette. 'Have you done Katharine Hepburn?'

'Is she alive?'

'Oh, yeah! She lives in New York. She's a really great lady. I'd love to have her as my friend. So I could call her up and . . . I don't know, just call her up.'

'I just interviewed Alanis Morissette. The singer.'

'Oh, she's sweet. She was at a party I went to last year in the canyons. This guy played "Rudolph the Red-Nosed Reindeer" with his cock on the piano. Really thumped the keys.' She frowned. 'It must have been Christmas.'

I gave a startled laugh. She seemed so naïve somehow – for all her crudeness, so childlike. Her radiance was magnetic. Yet she was surrounded by a darkness that puzzled me. 'Have you lived here for long?'

'Five years. But I'm going home to London. I like LA, but it's refu*gee* camp or something, if you're an actress. There are so many girls. And . . .' She shrugged. 'The men are all creeps.'

I said men were like that anywhere and she smiled. 'Some guys are okay,' she amended. 'They treat you like you might be a human being. It's the wives who are bitches.' She sighed. 'I know you're supposed to get used to it, but I can't. It really hurts.'

To our right the gate clanged again and a man appeared on the pink steps, silhouetted against the sun. He had white-grey hair and was decked out in a kind of glaring Chris Eubank snazziness: his belt shot flashes at the sun. He hurried sharply down the steps, his boots scraping the stone, and Patty's eyes darkened.

The man saw them – and bowled over. He stood over Patty so that his shadow blotted out her face. 'Where the hell have you been?'

She hunched her shoulders. 'Out.'

'For five days? Do you have any idea of the pressure I'm under?'

'Ed, this is –'

He didn't wait for the introduction. 'You'd better get your act together!' he warned furiously. 'Do you know how many agents are crawling round my office?'

'How is everything?' the plump waiter asked. He looked nervously from me to Patty, shorts flapping.

'Good,' snapped the man. He turned to block the waiter's view, his lips thin. 'We need to talk.'

'I don't want to.'

'I don't care what you goddamn want.'

He stalked to the next booth and waited impatiently. Patty bit her lip. Her neck was red and blotchy. 'I'm sorry,' she said. 'I didn't think he'd find me.'

'Who is he?'

'Ed Kaplan. My ex-boyfriend. I thought he'd got the message.'

'What message?'

But she had gone to the booth. I widened my eyes and picked up the paper. Ed Kaplan was clearly a tosser – the only question was why she had gone near him in the first place.

the Republicans, Kenneth Starr and now the Democrats have concentrated on the sexual scandals. There are a number of reasons for this. Any corrupt maladministration and fundraising would be extremely hard to prove. Of the twenty-one untimely deaths, five of them in plane crashes, it would be –

In the still air their voices carried quite clearly. 'A beer,' Kaplan told the waiter. 'And water.'

I was relieved that he seemed a bit calmer. He smoothed his hair with a plump, freckled hand. 'Look, I know you're upset that I couldn't see you.'

'Well, I think you could.'

'You know I couldn't. Betsey had plans. She'd already called.'

'Was that before or after I gave you the blow job?'

I gave an amused snort. Kaplan hunched his shoulders. 'Will you keep your *voice* down?'

But Patty leaned forward. 'I'm sick of this.'

'So am I. I told you –'

'*You* told me you were going to leave after the investigation!'

9

'And *I* said, because of the goddamn tax fiasco, that was blown out of the goddamn water!'

The waiter came up and they leaned back discontentedly. Kaplan raised a concessionary hand. 'Granted – I'm not going to leave her. But I tell you what I'll do. I'll get you out of that dump. And I'll get you a job. I'll talk to Arnold. And when this tax bullshit's –'

She drew away. 'I told you. It's too late!'

'Oh, for Christ's sake! You're impossible!'

I shook my head. What an arse! I disliked everything about him – his arrogance, his bullying, his paunch; his air of power – the smug creases on his hands.

'What do you *want*?' he was demanding. He eyed her with distaste. 'Is there *anything* that would make you happy?'

In the silence I heard a car accelerate, low, beyond the wall. Patty picked up her champagne and took a gulp. She set it down with a chink, as if she had come to a decision.

'Lots of things,' she said. 'You could try telling the truth. You could try not standing me up. You could leave your wife.' She shot him a malicious smile. 'You could get a bigger *cock*.'

My mouth opened. The man's gaze met mine absently: he didn't see me. 'You little bitch! When I've got the FB*I* on my tail –'

'I'm just telling the truth.'

'Well, I –!'

She touched her upper lip with her tongue. 'Oh

– and you could brush your teeth. Your breath smells like a sewer.'

He was quivering now like a whippet. His eyes narrowed with dislike. 'Joseph was right! You're just a two-timing little whore!'

I thought for a second he was going to hit her. But then he lowered his hand and slapped down some cash. His boots stabbed the concrete; his back bobbed up the steps like a pigeon's; the gate let out an almighty clang; and the only sound was the slow drip-drip of beer off the glass table.

Patty reached for her glass and took a swallow. Our eyes met. 'Guess I shouldn't have said that about his cock, huh?'

I tried not to smile. 'Guess not.'

'Hm.' Her gaze, less triumphant now, roamed the striped sunbeds. 'Still. I don't care.' She stood up and picked her way to our table. 'I'm going home anyway.'

'Exactly.'

'And he always like *wants* something. If I'm out, he has to know where I've been. If I'm on the phone I have to tell him who with.' She scrubbed at her arm. 'And he's never *there*. That's the worst thing. I wake up and this great emptiness sweeps over me. Do you get that?'

'Um, not quite.'

She pressed her hands to her stomach. 'It's like a pain *here*. All I want is a nice relationship. And I can't seem to get one. Why *is* that?'

She looked at me as if she genuinely expected an answer.

'Well, I'm sure you will –'

'But *when?*'

'You must have loads of men after you.'

'But I'm not *interested* in any of them. I don't know why Ed wouldn't marry me.'

'But he's married already!'

'But he's not happy! I saw his wife once, in Barney's. She was so thin and rich-looking. I felt like dog shit just looking at her.' She rubbed her bitten thumb gloomily at her lip, staring into the distance. 'Maybe I should call him.'

I stared. 'Don't you think you should –?'

'Move on?' She sighed. 'That's what Tyrone says. I just don't know what I do *wrong*. I try so hard and nothing ever works. Soon I'll be so old no one'll want to marry me. I'm already getting wrinkles. I wet myself if the bath's too hot. And look at my hands.'

But she thrust them in her lap as if to hide their inadequacy. 'At least my titties are okay. Sometimes I dance naked in front of the mirror. There's nothing wrong with *them.*'

I smiled and signed for the waiter. She seemed to have no shame: there seemed to be nothing she wouldn't say.

'Honestly,' I said. 'You're not *that* old.'

'I am, though! Thirty-one! How old are you?'

'Thirty-two.'

To our right the good-looking waiter, who'd been

12

on the phone to his mum, went and sat on a sunlounger, idly banging his wrists together. The plump one went up behind him, hesitated, put his hands in his pockets, and said in a low voice: 'So how's the smoking?'

Patty watched them as I dealt with the bill. 'I have to give up,' she said. She wiped her nose. 'I think I should stay quiet more.'

'Why?'

'I think guys like it. Joyce says I should stand up for myself.'

'Who's Joyce?'

'My friend. In London. Who I'm going to live with.'

'Oh, right.'

'She has a flat in Notting Hill Gate.'

'So do I!'

'No way!' She looked pleased. 'We can hang out!'

'Definitely.'

'Do *you* have a boyfriend?'

'Not really.' I shrugged. 'A commitmentphobe. A copywriter.'

'A what?'

'He works in advertising. He never tells me where he is. It's like going out with a piece of fog.'

'Oh, I know *that* feeling,' Patty exclaimed. 'Like when you ring the phone goes and goes even though you know they're there. Or you get through and they're really short, and you can hear them tapping on the computer, not really listening.' She lit a cigarette. 'Does yours stay the night?'

'Once in a blue moon.'

'See, Ed was a Scorpio,' Patty remarked. 'I think that was the problem. But when I went to this psychic last year, in Los Feliz, she said I wouldn't marry my current boyfriend. So I knew it wouldn't last.'

'You believed her?'

'Oh she's really good! She does all the stars!'

That afternoon, with the sunlight shimmering on the restless pool and the fountain splashing over the low purr of the traffic, I felt for the first time the gilded, dreamlike promise of that desert city. Even when one of the waiters began polishing the plastic leaves of the bougainvillea it all seemed magical, enchanting.

So did Patty, with her agonised mixture of radiance and doubt. And though even then I sensed the unacknowledged doom that seemed to hover round her, I had no inkling of the storms she would trigger, or the far-reaching consequences of our meeting, which would transform all our lives.

'Have you ever had a relationship you really wanted to work out,' she asked me then, 'and it never did?'

'All the time.'

She grinned, but her eyes met the horizon with a tearful gleam. 'I tell you my problem,' she said. 'I'm just magnetically attracted to cunts.'

We climbed the pink steps. At the top three Mexicans were clearing a flowerbed, troughing in a dark pool of dirt. They worked with a strange urgency, sweating in the heat. Patty stared at them, her face solemn.

'Do you ever feel nostalgic,' she asked, 'like the best is over, and you're missing something important, but you don't know what it is?'

Then the foyer's dark chill closed over us.

'I'm so excited,' Patty said. 'When I get to London the first thing I'm going to do is –'

Her face changed and I turned to see Ed Kaplan.

Patty scrubbed at her eye and said, 'Ed.'

He came up to her and they looked at each other for a long moment – a strange look, indecipherable. 'I got us a room,' he said.

She hunched her shoulders. *'No!'*

'You won't come?'

'I don't *want* to!' She stamped her foot.

'My little girl.' He reached for her head; touched her hair. I saw she stood still under his embrace – that her body seemed to yearn towards it. 'I've missed you,' he murmured.

'You're just saying that.'

'I love you.'

He leaned closer, his thumb to her lips. 'I got your favourite room.'

She swallowed.

'I got your favourite champagne.'

I stepped forward. 'Patty?'

But she shook her head, a gesture of warning.

They went to the lift. I stared in dismay. Was this some kind of ritual? Was she in danger? Or did

15

they always fight and make up? Other people were watching them too – or her. A man in rimless glasses was openly staring: his eyes went up and down her body, over the sweat circles under her arms, the damp tendrils on her neck.

Kaplan had pressed the button of the lift. He said something to Patty, but I didn't catch her reply. The lift opened with a ping. They slid from sight.

CHAPTER 2

That afternoon, at the airport, I worried about Patty and even tried to call her. But I didn't get through. At Heathrow I tried again – no reply. When I got home it was too late in the evening to ring. Then it began to seem weird to try, as the days went by and the memory of our encounter receded. Plus, I had my own problems: specifically, the commitmentphobe copywriter and family difficulties involving a court case. After a while the memory of that afternoon and its unsatisfactory ending faded and the practicalities of my life overlaid it, like sea washing over sand.

So it took me a second to place her when she rang. It was a Friday late in January, midwinter, that bleak moment when the trees are brown sticks on a white sky, and Clinton's impeachment trial had begun – his enemies had got his head. 'Hey,' she said. 'Bet you don't remember me,' and I was thrown back to the Beverly Hills Hotel, and the hot sunshine on my parting, and the languid air of dirt and decay. 'My God,' I said, 'how are you?'

I had forgotten that clear voice, too, that created instant intimacy with its candid confessions.

'I'm really good,' she said. 'Isn't England fun? I'm so happy to be back' – and she said a lot more when we met the following afternoon at the new Starbucks on Oxford Street. She looked different and after a minute I realised why: she wasn't wearing make-up. But her eyes shone and she simmered with the same vitality I had found so captivating in LA.

I smiled. 'So you came back.'

She wriggled her shoulders. 'I did. I can't believe it. I'm so happy. Everyone's so lovely.' She prised the top off her latte and I remembered what else I had forgotten: those ugly hands, marred by tiny red lines. 'And it's so pretty! I'd forgotten. I went for a walk in the park yesterday and I was just running, it was so magical: the pond and the dogs and everything.' She buried her mouth in her coffee and swallowed, smiling. 'It feels like some children's story: you know, a fairy tale – Narnia, or something.'

'I wish I had your optimism.' I smiled to take the edge off this and took a sip of coffee. 'So when did you come back? What happened with your boyfriend?'

'Boyfriend?' Her eyes went blank. 'Oh! Ed.' She sucked her coffee. 'How'd you know about him?'

'The last I saw he was frogmarching you to a lift. I was worried.'

'Oh!' She licked her lip. 'Yes. Gosh.'

'I tried to call you.'

'Did you? Oh.'

'So what happened?'

She shrugged. 'Nothing. I mean. We just hung out for a bit. But guess what? I've got a new boyfriend. He's *lovely*. Really sexy.' She grinned. 'You have to meet him.'

'I'd like to.'

'And I'm sharing a flat.'

'With Joyce.'

'Shit, you've got a good memory. Mine's terrible. I can't remember a thing.'

They lived in Linden Gardens. We talked about that for a while – Joyce was a yoga teacher who had danced with the Bolshoi – and then the conversation turned back to men and marriage. Patty seemed to view it as a holy grail. She seemed to feel that it would redeem her, or save her, like some kind of charm.

'It isn't that great, you know,' I told her pompously. 'You don't need a guy to feel complete.'

'But I do,' Patty said simply. 'I'm much happier with a guy. Having someone to sleep next to – someone to give you a hug when you're down. And not having to go places on your own, and having someone to carry your suitcase. Linda, my psychic, said I'd be married next year.' She grinned hopefully. 'He's going to be blond and tall, with a May birthday.'

'That cuts down the field.'

'The trouble is Ramzi's dark and was born in

19

July. Joyce thinks I'm nuts anyway to want to get married – she says men always let you down.' She sighed. 'Ed sure did.'

'Well, that's over.'

'Mm.' She sighed again, her fingers plucking her skirt. 'I kind of miss him though. I keep thinking about when we got together. We went to Napa and had a picnic in this vineyard and he told me about when he was a little boy – he had this really sad childhood, and –' she shrugged. 'He was really sweet.'

'Well, now you've got Ramzi.'

Her face lightened. 'That's true. He's really kind of definite. I like that. He knows what he wants. We spent the whole of yesterday in bed.'

'What does he do?'

'He's a salesman. You'll never guess what he said yesterday. That I was the sexiest girl he'd ever seen.'

A man in a thick blue overcoat came up to us. 'Excuse me. I just wanted to say that you are absolutely beautiful.'

'Oh! Thank you!'

'No, thank *you*.'

'Wasn't that sweet?' Patty asked. She smiled radiantly. 'I just feel so happy at the moment. Like roses are going to fall all round me.'

'So he sells things?'

'Huh? Oh. Yes. And, um. He has a Porsche. Which he drives really fast. And he can get tables everywhere. Which reminds me: do you want to go shopping? Ramzi said my bra looked like it was from Goodwill.'

Heads turned and a bus driver honked as Patty hustled over Oxford Street. 'The thing about underwear,' she observed, as she queued for the changing rooms, 'is the minute you turn thirty you get a *craving* for it. Like coke. Except I hate coke-heads. They're so unimaginative. At least smackies are poetic.'

She wandered into a cubicle and began undressing, not bothering to draw the curtain. 'When I'm married,' she said, 'I'm going to cook. I'm going to have a big country kitchen. And a study. And a grandfather clock.'

'Well, there's no rush.'

'There *is*! I'm getting wrinkles! I'm running out of *time*! Oh, this one's sexy.'

She materialised topless in front of me, in a pair of shocking pink lace knickers.

'Patty!'

'What? It's only titties.' She stepped into her cubicle. 'Ramzi says he might get married if he meets the right girl,' she went on, more muffled. 'But he doesn't like to be pinned down – he hates people telling him what to do. Oh, I like this one.'

She re-emerged, this time clothed. 'And he's *unbelievable* in bed. Better than anyone.'

'Where did you meet?'

'At LAX.' She walked to the till, dangling a yellow bra. 'I'm going to get this. It reminds me of buttercups: we had a field of them behind our house. Yeah, so it was really weird. I was at LAX, drinking a glass of Moët, because I was kind of sad, in a way, to be leaving. I'd had a bunch of fun there, and I hadn't got anywhere: I wasn't this great big star. And I was thinking I was getting old, and about Ed, because we used to drink there, and wishing someone would rescue me, like a white knight on a charger, when he came up and said "hi".'

Her face lit with remembered joy; the woman at the checkout, matronly, with grey hair, gave a startled smile. 'And he put down his beer and said, "There are only three reasons a beautiful woman looks sad at an airport. The first is that her husband is having an affair. The second is she is leaving her lover. And the third"' – she frowned. 'I can't remember the third.' She took the bag. '*Thank* you. Then he bought a whole bottle of Moët, and we got talking, and he was just really, really nice. He said the same as you, by the way, about Ed – that I was better off without him.'

'I bet he did.'

'And he was really sweet about me leaving LA. He said I was bound to get better parts in England, because there was less competition. Not in a bad way. He could see how serious I was about acting.'

She stepped onto the escalator, placing her bitten hand on the rail. 'And then we slept together and it was brilliant. We had this instant connection.'

'Wow. Straightaway?'

'In the disabled toilet. It was pretty big. And we sat together on the flight. He had a first-class ticket, but he came to sit in economy. He's English. He lives in London.'

'God. That's – that's fast.'

'How do you mean?' Patty's face pinched and darkened; she folded her arms.

'Well: nothing. Just that it was – fast.'

She walked to the next escalator. Every part of her seemed to droop: I felt terrible. 'Sorry,' I said. 'I didn't mean to upset you.'

She hugged herself, frowning. 'I'm not.'

But she was. 'What about a glass of champagne?' I coaxed. 'To say sorry?'

'I don't know.'

'Go on. You haven't told me about his star sign yet.'

'That's true,' she said. She shot me a look and she giggled.

We went to an Italian place on Duke Street. They didn't have any cold champagne, so we drank it with lumps of ice at the bar.

She looked round happily. 'This is fun,' she said. 'Kind of like being on location. If you like being on location. Which I most certainly don't.'

'Why not?'

'The directors are psychos. And you always have an affair.' She took a meditative sip. 'You make some good friends, though. On my last one a cameraman called Charlie gave me an amazing book. Have you read *Daisy Miller*?'

23

'Not for ages.'

'Oh, you should. It's amazing. It's about this girl who dies because no one in society'll speak to her. It's just terrible.'

'I thought it was more because she didn't follow the rules of society?'

'No, no, everyone is really mean to her. She's like an angel and this rich man falls in love with her and everything – I cried buckets at the end.'

'Well, I should re-read it.'

'Charlie gave me a book about dreams, too, that's incredible. Because I was having all these terrible dreams – that I was getting blinded in all these different ways, like a knife was going through my eye and a red-hot poker and everything – really bad. And the book said that dreams were like letters from your soul – you had to read them like they're emails from a distant lover. It said people try and ignore their spiritual core, but it never goes away, and dreams guide us back to it.'

'Goodness.'

She nibbled her thumb. 'You're laughing at me.'

'I'm not!'

'You are. You're laughing inside. And that's the worst kind of laugh.'

I grinned. 'It's just – I'm not a believer in all that stuff. That dreams have some kind of deep message. But I suppose it could be true.'

'Oh, it is,' she said. 'In sleep, you see, you dissolve into the wholeness of Creation. So you *have* to understand your dreams.'

'So what was your soul trying to say about being blinded?'

'I've no idea!' She stared, wide-eyed. 'That's why I read the book!'

The dusk thickened and spread. In the neon streetlit gloom Patty sank her chin into her hand. 'It's the kind of night you should go home to a boyfriend,' she mused. 'Sit by a fire with your head in his lap, knowing you've just got out of bed and in a minute you'll go back. I want to be buried on a night like this – by my kids, if I have any.'

'That's rather morbid.'

'I don't think so. I like the idea of dying. It's cosy somehow; nothing can bother you any more; and you won't ever get old.' She sighed meditatively, and I was reminded of my thought the first time I met her – that she was surrounded by a confounding darkness. 'I used to plan my funeral.'

'Heavens, why?'

'I don't know.' She tucked her hair behind her ear. 'Joyce doesn't like him.'

'Who?'

'Ramzi.'

'Why not?'

'I don't know. She's funny about my boyfriends. She didn't like Ed either.'

It seemed to be worrying her, but before I could ask her more the waiter came up. 'Another?' he enquired. He looked her up and down with a furtive, guilty lust. 'Bella, you are one bee-yootiful girl.'

★　　★　　★

25

Getting to know someone happens by degrees. You learn their history, meet their partner, family, friends; see how they react to crises, find out their opinions. If you have discrimination you act in response to these events and step back or come forward. It was one of Patty's tragedies that she had no ability to discriminate. If someone was abusive, or selfish, or violent, she took it – because she didn't know any better. She didn't see when people treated her like shit, and she didn't see when they treated her well. She didn't see when they were in love with her – and she didn't see when she was driving them mad.

But I didn't know that then. That evening, sitting next to Patty on a swerving 23 bus, I had the feeling I had had on summer nights at university – that life stretched ahead forever, golden with joy. She must have felt the same, because when we got to Notting Hill she clutched my arm and begged me to come home with her.

'Please.'

'Aren't you meeting Ramzi?'

'No, he's working. Do. You can see my room.'

'I should really get back.'

'And then I can show you a picture.'

We crossed the Bayswater Road. Patty's street huddled under an orange sky, the 'for sale' signs bristling. She buzzed the front door, and walked through to a shabby hallway dotted with dusty piles of post addressed in elaborate writing to people with unpronounceable names. Dirt streaked the skirting boards. On the second floor a narrow door swung open to reveal a woman who scrutinised us with alert sleepy eyes.

She had spongy red hair drawn into a plait, a hollow, bony face, and wide shoulders: she must have been six feet tall. Her skirt ended in a knotted fringe under a leotard that cupped her wrinkled breasts; her feet were bare. She was around fifty, and there was something insidiously intriguing about her: you looked at her again.

'There you are,' she said in a husky voice. 'I've been taking calls for you all day. Where's your key?'

'I forgot it,' Patty said. 'We've been shopping. You'll never guess what I got.'

'I don't suppose I shall.'

'A bra.' She smiled eagerly. 'This is Joyce. Joyce, this is Lottie.'

'Hello Lottie,' said Joyce, turning an unemotional gaze on me. She turned back to Patty. 'So did you see Steve?'

'Just for a minute.'

'Did he ask you?'

'Oh gosh. I can't remember. Let me show you my bra.'

Patty went through a doorway and began undressing, dropping her clothes on the floor. That body! It was like a plum about to fall. There was something so innocent about her desire to show it you couldn't be offended; she was like a child turning a cartwheel on the grass.

Joyce watched impassively, and then turned to me.

27

'I hear you're a journalist.'

'That's right.'

'Who do you write for?'

'Mainly *The Times*.'

She raised her eyebrows. She said to Patty: 'I thought I asked you to tidy up.'

Her room was certainly a mess. Clothes strewed the bed. Mugs of tea mouldered on speakers. An open pot of cream had been used as an ashtray. Yellowing scripts gathered dust by the bed. A pair of knickers lay on the floor by Joyce's foot.

'I wondered where those had gone,' Joyce said with studied neutrality. She bent and picked up a pair of tweezers. 'Do you know how much these cost?'

'Sorry,' Patty said. She turned, smiling hopefully. 'So what do you think?'

Joyce bent down again. 'I wondered why we didn't have anything to drink out of. How long have these been here?'

'Not long. Don't you love it?'

'Very nice.'

'Let's celebrate. Let's have champagne.'

'We don't have any. You and Ramzi drank it.'

'Did we?'

'Yes.'

'Oh. Well, he'll get some more.'

'Good,' Joyce said. She went off down the corridor and we burst into giggles.

'What's her problem?' I said.

Patty bit her lip and shut the door. 'She's sweet

really. She just gets jealous. She's been really kind to me – a real tough old granny. I went to her because I had these pains in my ovaries, and she started helping me with all sorts of other things – I've got blocks in my hips, she says, from all my bad relationships. She's ever so wise.'

'How old is she?'

'She says forty. But really fifty-two. I saw her passport.'

She got up and began rooting through an Indonesian chest that leaned at an angle from the wall. The room was small and square, with a disproportionately low ceiling. A red cotton curtain drooped from a broom handle doubling as a makeshift curtain rail. Behind it was a crumbling windowsill. The impression was of dreary dated-ness, not quite poverty.

'Look,' said Patty. She looked down with an unreadable expression. 'Isn't he handsome?'

It was a sun-yellowed snapshot of a couple. He had matinee idol looks, a broad smile, and the knowing twinkle of a crooked salesman about to clinch a deal. She was homely, her smile resigned.

'Your parents?'

'Mm.' She touched the head of the man gently.

'He looks like a charmer.'

'Oh, he was. Could charm the birds off the trees.'

'I'm going to make moussaka,' Joyce said, opening the door. 'I'd offer you some, Lottie, but I expect you've got plans.'

Patty smiled. 'Oh gosh. Actually, I have to go out.'

'What, now?'

Patty just stared at her sweetly, not replying.

'Well, if you change your mind,' Joyce said in a dissatisfied tone. 'By the way, have you seen my silver necklace?'

'I had it last night. Didn't I put it back?'

'No, you didn't.'

'Oh! It's here.' Patty retrieved a clanking object from the floor.

'Thanks.' She disappeared into the hall; the door closed with a click.

We looked at each other and grinned.

'Funny, isn't she?' said Patty. 'Let's go to yours.'

'What, now?'

'Why not?'

'I don't know. Well. Okay. I thought you had plans?'

She gave me a little shrug. 'I think sometimes she wants to *eat* me. Come on. Let's hurry.'

As we tiptoed out I caught a glimpse of Joyce in the kitchen, carving cling film with a serrated knife. She didn't hear us over the music – she was singing along to Jane Birkin, crooning really, in tuneless French.

In those days I lived in a house in Artesian Road – part of that grid of stucco streets that runs behind Westbourne Grove. I had been left it by my aunt and had never liked it – it was dark on the ground floor and chill, like a church. In my depressed state of mind it didn't occur to me to move; Patty, for her part, was impressed.

'This is huge,' she breathed. 'You didn't say you were rich.'

'I'm not really. It's not as big as it looks.'

She went into the dining room; peered at the invitations. 'Do you live on your own?'

'Mm-hm.'

'Don't you get lonely?'

'Not really.'

'Wow.' She was examining the pictures on the kitchen wall. 'Are these your parents?'

'Mm-hm.'

'Your mum looks nice. Does she always wear hats?'

'Not really.'

'Is that your dad?'

'Mm-hm.'

'He looks really masterful. He reminds me of Ed.'

'He walked out on us when I was five,' I said. 'His girlfriend's younger than I am. He's pretty dysfunctional.'

'Oh, really,' Patty said. She looked at him with more interest. 'I don't know anyone whose parents are still together. Apart from Tyrone's, of course.' She hopped up on the counter. 'His parents have sex still, all the time. The last time he went home they were doing it in the bathroom. That's the kind of marriage I want. I think I could with Ramzi.

He likes sex. He's clever, too. He loves to read.' She scrambled off the counter to get a cigarette. 'But guess what he told me last night? He was born with such bad eczema he bled. He spent his whole first year covered in bandages. Can you imagine? His mum sounds like such a bitch. She used to hit him.'

I gave her an ashtray and opened my hoarded bottle of Cloudy Bay and as she chattered I felt an elemental warmth spreading through me. I wasn't used to company in my kitchen; my life had become solitary; separate. I would eat at the kitchen table, staring at the wet paving stones, or a Victorian novel. Then I would go upstairs and work on my novel, or read psychology books. *Understanding The Tin Man* was the latest one I had bought in an attempt, vain, to penetrate the psyche of the copywriter.

'Oh, I love those,' Patty said. 'Have you read *The Road Less Travelled?* That's brilliant. It's like therapy, only better.'

'Have you had therapy?'

'No. Well; once. But she was really weird: she smoked all time, and had these big yellowy teeth. She kept saying I was late, when I wasn't – I used to get so nervous about being on time. And she kept going on about my dad abandoning me. Well, he didn't – he got sent to jail.' She frowned as if a thought had just occurred to her. 'D'you think Joyce is lesbian?'

'Very possibly.'

'Because I woke up the other night and found her by the bed staring at me.'

'Oh my God.'

'I know!' She yawned. 'So are you from London?'

'Mm-hm. And Scotland.'

She nodded. 'And now your dad's seeing someone else? See, that's the trouble with older men. When my dad got out of jail he started seeing this nineteen-year-old and she always took the front seat in the car. You can tell a lot about someone if they always take the front seat.'

'Was he there for long?'

She shook her head. 'He was a conman. So my mum moved to Vegas. She always wanted to be a croupier.'

'And was she?'

'Uh-huh.'

'But she came back?'

'When she broke up with her boyfriend.'

'And where is she now?'

'In a home.'

'Oh. I'm sorry.'

'That's okay. Are you hungry?'

'Starving. Are you?'

We ordered a takeaway. I lit candles and opened another bottle of wine, and we talked into the night. The conversation was so easy that when at midnight she yawned, 'It's so nice here – I don't want to go home,' it seemed like the most natural thing in the world to invite her to stay. But I felt awkward and clumsy as a balloon as we made up the bed – it had been so long since I had had anyone sleep over.

'I like it here,' she said, snuggling under the covers as the sash snapped and rattled in the wind. 'It's homey. It smells of shells.'

'Dust, more like.'

'No, shells.' She smiled at me trustingly. 'I'm glad that we're friends.'

CHAPTER 3

I came down the next morning to find Patty perched at the kitchen table. The mess of the night before had been cleared away – roughly speaking – and a posy of pinched rosebuds, the last from my garden, was set at my place beside an ornate green and white china eggcup that must have belonged to my aunt.

Alongside them lay a copy of *Hello!*, a pack of Minstrels, and *The Times* – SCANDAL IN THE WHITE HOUSE:

> He has lied, cheated and defied justice for twenty years. It no longer matters whether the President apologises yet again or has himself flogged on the steps of the Capitol. Theatrics cannot save him.

'Hi!' cried Patty. 'Look what I've got. D'you like Minstrels? And *Hello!*, for your research. And *The Times*, from the front door. Look, there's a picture of Nicole Kidman. And I got eggs and everything. I'm going to boil you one now.'

She began battering a pan with cold water. 'I

slept so well. I think it was because I wasn't with Joyce. The blankets were so heavy. I felt all safe, like at my Nan's when I was little. And the view from that window is so pretty. With all that snow.'

'It's snowing?' I went yawning to the French doors. It was, a little – thin flakes circling like gnats in the air. 'God, I'm hungover. How much did we drink?'

'Two bottles,' Patty said. 'Maybe three. And someone rang. With a surprised-sounding voice.'

'My mother.'

'She said could you ring back as soon as you get up, please, because she has to go to Christie's. Kirsty's.'

'Christie's.'

'And there's a cat wanting breakfast. I thought I'd better ask before letting him in.'

A ginger tom was huddled on the path; when it saw me it leapt to its feet and began rubbing sinuously against the glass. 'Oh, Lord,' I said. 'That thug.'

'He's sweet!' Patty cried. She tapped the glass and the cat bared its throat in a soundless meow. 'Look! He's talking to us.'

'He'll probably *eat* us.'

I let it in. Released from its purdah the cat began throwing itself, with great knocking pushes of its shoulder, at Patty's leg. She scooped it up and opened the Minstrels. 'I had such a funny dream,' she said. 'I dreamed Joyce was running at me with a knife. And then Ed came out of a bush and kissed me and I was petrified: I knew I was going to die.'

'A Judas kiss.'

'A what?'

'A Judas kiss. As in the Last Supper. You know, Christ.'

'Oh, right.' She blinked. 'And it's so weird, because he called yesterday.'

'Who did?'

'Ed.'

I stared. 'You didn't *talk* to him?'

'Well – just for a second.'

'Patty!'

'No, but he was really sweet. He said he wanted me back – he missed me – his life was falling apart.'

'But he's still married, right?'

'Well, yes.'

'So you're best out of it.'

'Do you think?' She nibbled her thumb. 'I suppose so. And he does have a temper – phew! You don't want to be near *him* when he's cross. Once he thought I'd lost his briefcase and he went nutty. I thought he was going to *strangle* me.'

'That's really not cool, Patty.'

'I know. And he used to tell me I was an idiot and my bum was huge – and that I dressed like a whore.'

'Charming!'

'I know.' She took another Minstrel. 'And someone else rang. Jean-Pierre? He said to tell you one-thirty pm.' She wiped her mouth deli-cately. 'He sounded nice.'

'He *is* nice. He was at university with me.' I smiled. 'I'm going to lunch at his.'

'What does he do?'

'He's a journalist. He's amazing. His wife's amazing too.'

'He's married?'

'*Mm-hm.*' I got up to take out my egg. 'To Simone.'

'Oh.' She rubbed at her nose. 'He invited me, actually.'

'He did?' I turned and stared. 'Well – come then.'

'Really?'

'Sure. If you like. But it's in Sussex. It's a two-hour drive.'

'Really?'

'Well . . . yes. Why not? You can map-read.'

Which was how it began.

Snow crouched like puppies on the trees as we drove out of London, and in the brown monochrome countryside the windows of Jean-Pierre Clark's farmhouse seemed to glow yellow with hope. He was alone when we arrived, stacking logs by the fire-place, and he rose heavily, brushing bark from his jersey, his air of weariness just strong enough to cut his charm. He had had his hair cut, and his hacked head made him look like a badly shorn sheep. That day, I noticed what I always noticed: his thick, sensual lips, small hands and missing earlobe.

38

Away from him, his weariness was what lingered in your mind; with him, you just wanted him to be in love with you. It wasn't just me who felt that way – it was every woman I knew. His attraction, I had concluded, came from his combination of sophistication and his aloofness: he had an iron-clad self-possession. His family were rich: his mother lived with his stepfather in the South of France; his father owned a night-club in Chelsea.

Jean-Pierre never talked about them, though I had met his mother once at university – she had quick dark eyes, a throaty laugh and wore Chanel. He was very fond of her, as far as I could tell: he was almost impossible to read, and always gave the impression that he had reached conclusions about people that he wasn't going to reveal. He was one of those people who had been everywhere and done everything, a complicated man who seemed to yearn, in an almost poignant way, to be good.

'I've turned into a country gentleman,' he said now, coming forward. 'I even chop wood. How was the drive?'

'Very good.'

'I hope you won't freeze. We've been nannying fires all morning.'

He took Patty's hand with a muffled flash of surprise at her beauty. 'Take a seat. I'll hunt down drinks. We had Simone's family for Christmas, which was not unlike having a platoon of soldiers billeted on you in the war.'

At either end the room swelled into bay windows, the delicate glass distorted with ancient flaws. Brooding yews marked out the snow-blank garden. Squatting incongruously on the grey marble mantel-piece were two African figures, faces clenched in the agony of birth.

'So what's your news?' Jean-Pierre asked, ferrying a tray of wine and glasses. 'Copywriter behaving?'

'Of course not.'

'I saw him somewhere.' He set down the bottle. 'Oh, Soho House.' He looked at Patty. 'Chablis okay?'

'Um. Sure.'

She was sitting slightly forward with her hands clasped on her knees.

Jean-Pierre poured a glass, gave it to her, and stepped back, as from a fire. 'We saw a play with Mark David last night,' he said. 'And Christine.'

'How was that?'

'Pretty bad. Mark was on good form.'

'What play?' Patty asked.

He glanced at her. '*Sleep With Me*. At the National.'

'Hanif Kureishi?'

He raised his eyebrows. 'That's right.'

'I read about that.'

'Well, it's not very good.'

'But with an awful honesty,' said Simone. She had come in at the far end of the room without my noticing; now she hurried towards us, wiping her hands on her hips. 'Lottie! How lovely you could come. Excuse my filthy nails. I look like a stable-hand.'

She was a photographer, and had met Jean-Pierre in Bosnia, where he was reporting on the war.

'This is Patty.'

'Hello! How nice to meet you!'

Simone's smile promised compassion, and I could see Patty blossoming in it like a flower in the sun. Her magnolia beauty made Simone's face look rough, coarse – until you saw her eyes. Mark had once told me they had the most depth he had ever seen; but it was the kindness in them that I always noticed, and the warmth.

'I *love* your jumper,' Patty told her.

'I love yours,' Simone said. She smiled at Jean-Pierre.

Patty lit up. 'Oh, thanks! I got it from Hennes. They have such good things. Really cheap. You can get loads of stuff for five pounds. Four, even.'

'Can you?'

'Oh, yes! I went in the other day, after an audition, and got seven things. Really cheap – you should go! I'll come with you if you like.'

'There's an idea. I never go shopping.'

'Oh, I'm a great shopper!'

'Well, have a drink,' Jean-Pierre said. He put a hand on Simone's back. 'How's the soup?'

'Simmering.' She grinned at me. 'I'm experimenting. I hope it's edible. How's the copywriter?'

'Terrible.'

'You should go out with Mark David.'

'He wouldn't look at me!'

As if on cue a door slammed, two voices blended in the distance, and Mark David appeared in the doorway. He raised a hand. 'Sorry. The traffic was diabolical.'

'I tried to get him to leave earlier,' Christine lamented, sighing up behind. 'I *said* it would be terrible. Breakdown on the A40, miles and miles of queues, and then we ran out of petrol . . .'

She came tiptoeing to Simone, her face contorted to indicate the intensity of their nightmare.

'Lottie,' Mark said in his light, dry voice.

He had also been at university with us. Tall, stiff, reserved, with a bony, sensitive face, he had an upright respectability that was at odds with his colourful parentage. His mother, who had run off with an Argentinian polo player, had married five times in all – she was an alcoholic. His father wrote poetry and was a priest in Wales. Mark seemed to take after him. He had got the top first in our year, where he was regarded as a genius, and become a hugely successful playwright. I had always felt intimidated by him. He made me feel inherently messy. I think this was more to do with him than me: at college I once overheard someone remark that he looked like he was rigid with inhibition.

Christine was his first and only girlfriend. He stuck with her despite the fact that she was far less intelligent than him and less attractive – one of her unappealing qualities was that, limpet-like, she would never let him go. She had gone to Oxford poly, and had met him at a Christchurch ball – they had been together ever since.

'This is Patty,' I told them.

'How do you do?' Mark asked. His eyes grazed her cleavage and he blushed.

'*Hi!*' Christine cried. She held her hand to Patty and shuddered theatrically. 'I've had such dreadful flu. I've been blowing my nose all *week*.' She let her jaw drop sharply to show her frustration.

'Was I imagining it,' Mark said to Jean-Pierre, 'or was last night's play a rehash of *Intimacy*?'

'It was a rehash of *Intimacy*,' Jean-Pierre said.

'He has such a sharp mind. It's a great shame.'

'I just saw *A Streetcar Named Desire*,' Patty said. She smiled round trustfully. 'It was amazing.'

'You did?' Mark enquired. He stared at her with a peculiar expression, as if sucking ice cream. 'Are you fond of the theatre?'

'I love it. Tennessee Williams especially. He's so deep down and dirty. But that's what life's like, isn't it? Poor Blanche, relying on the comfort of strangers. I feel like her sometimes.'

'I'm sure not.' He cleared his throat. 'What do you do?'

'I'm an actress. I make movies. They're always turkeys.' She looked round – saw she had our attention. 'But, you know, it's a start; and one day I might be famous. You know when you want something so bad you can *see* it? That's how I feel

43

about acting. I used to dream about it. I used to think if I wished hard enough my wish would come true and I would be there, up on stage with Mamet, and Kazan.'

'Well,' said Jean-Pierre kindly, when the silence had stretched on, 'perhaps we should eat.'

As we filed into the hall I saw a grey cat break from the cover of the yews, its back low with fear, its fur flattened in the breeze.

'Oh, thanks,' Patty said, blushing, when Mark pulled out her chair.

'You can admire our colour-scheme,' said Jean-Pierre. 'We got carried away.'

'I *like* it,' Simone said.

We stared at the deep red walls.

'It's quite dark, isn't it?' Christine said. 'Personally, I prefer blue for a dining room. Have you tried the Paint Library on Elystan Street? They do some pretty blues.'

'I'm sure they can decide for themselves,' Mark told her.

'I was only *saying*.'

We ate pumpkin soup. Patty watched carefully as everyone picked up their spoon, then followed suit.

Jean-Pierre filled our glasses. 'We're celebrating,' he said. 'Simone's up for the Deutsche Prize.'

'Darling,' Simone said. She shook her head smiling.

'It's true.' He smiled at her. 'My wife's officially a genius.'

'Ignore him!'

'She even cooks.'

'I *try* to cook.'

'Simone saved a man's life,' I told Patty. 'Towed him to shore with her bra.'

'Heavens!' Simone cried. She picked up the ladle. 'Who's for more soup?'

'Gosh. I can't think of anything better,' Patty said. 'Than to save a man's life.'

'I didn't, really,' Simone said. 'The water was shallow.'

'But still! I bet he was so grateful.'

The sun glistened on the snow and glanced off Mark's glasses as he watched Patty eat. 'It's good to see a girl with an appetite,' he told her as she finished her second helping.

'Oh, I hoover food. I'm like a bottom feeder.'

'Well, you look well on it.'

'I think it's great about the *prize*,' Christine said. She put a hand on Mark's arm. 'Mark and I have been meaning to take some more pictures. Haven't we? We put a lovely album together of Venice.'

After lunch we walked up the Downs on an icy track rutted with hoof-prints. The wind whistled in our ears and the sheep's breath smoked as they stared at us sideways.

Patty was quiet on the way home. 'How long have they been married?' she asked.

'Who, Jean-Pierre and Simone? Three years.'

'She's not very pretty.'

'No, but she's wonderful.'

45

'I mean I liked her,' she said consideringly. 'But I'd never put them together. She's quite – earth mother-ish.'

'She's very wise, though. She's very *loving*.'

'Is he clever?'

'Jean? Yes. Quite. Worldly, really. His family lost all their money in Lloyd's.'

'What's Lloyd's?'

'An insurance thing. He's very honourable. Women always fall for him.'

'Do they?'

'He used to go out with a beautiful Russian model.'

'What happened?'

'He got sick of the scenes, I think. And he met Simone.'

'And – what's his name – Mark David? Has he been with that girl for long?'

'Twelve years. Tragically.'

'Why?'

'Because she's so ghastly. She's his first girl-friend.'

She fell silent all the rest of the way, until I pulled up at Joyce's flat. Then she said: 'So he's always like that?'

'Who?'

'Jean-Pierre.'

'Like what?'

'I don't know. He seemed – funny.'

I shrugged. 'He seemed fine to me.'

★   ★   ★

I had met Simone Clark in the South of France. Crimson bougainvillea had hung behind the long plastic table. The sun had glittered on the blue rug of the sea, tiny white sailboats creeping across it, leaning forward.

It was my friend Rupert's mother's villa near Mougins. I had dropped in for a lunch party. Fifteen or so people, and one of them Jean-Pierre. He was just back from Sarajevo, and the second I saw him I knew something had changed. The thousands of muscles in his face seemed to have reconfigured. He looked quite different – young, boyish, relaxed. I knew it must be because of his new girlfriend – we all knew he was in love.

And I remembered my shock when Jean-Pierre picked up the hand of the woman sitting next to him: the homely brunette. She was dark with a thick waist. Her eyebrows were heavy and unplucked. It was those that struck me most: by then everyone plucked their eyebrows. I thought: *She's ugly.*

Then she smiled at him and my stomach lurched because their trust and love were so obvious in the brilliant Mediterranean sunshine.

'Lottie!' Jean-Pierre cried, and got up, smiling self-consciously. He kissed me and I smelt his sun cream and felt his familiar air of ease and entitlement, and his faint defensiveness, which hadn't gone. He stuck his hands in his pockets.

'How are you?'

'Well. And you?'

'Very good.' He shuffled his feet. 'I have some news.'

'I heard! You met someone. That's great!'

He gave me a penetrating look. 'She is great.'

'Ah,' the woman exclaimed, hurrying up from her chair, and I saw that her legs were dark with long hairs. 'Hello!'

'Hi there,' I said. I put my hand up to shade my eyes.

She moved so I could see her. 'It's so nice to meet you! I'm Simone. Have you come to stay?'

'No, no. Just for lunch.'

'Well, that's great! I've read your pieces. They're fantastic.'

I cleared my throat. 'So are you here for long?'

'In France? No. A couple of days. I'd love to stay, but' she put out her square hand. 'Work calls.'

I nodded. 'Well, it's nice to meet you.'

She put out her hand. 'You too.'

I watched her through lunch. She was just herself, looking seriously at whoever she was talking to, laughing a deep belly laugh. Fragments of her conversation floated to me. Once she began talking to the man next to her about Bosnia. He contradicted her, and she laughed, shook her head, and flicked her hand in a gesture of dismissal. When she stood I saw her thick ankles above unflattering sandals. Her denim dress strained around her hips.

Jean-Pierre looked at her as if she might vanish. 'Like her?' he asked.

'Very much.'

He nodded as if there were no other possible reply.

'How did you meet?'

'I nearly ran her over. By the Holiday Inn. She was with Nagi, whose parents had been killed. She was furious with me. I persuaded her to have a drink. She was taking pictures for *Le Monde*.'

'I'd never have put you two together.'

'Yes. I finally grew up.'

He had the air of a man who had overcome a great challenge, one that he had feared he might fail.

'She's a photographer?'

'Took the first pictures of the siege. I'll show you. They're incredible.'

'Was she there throughout the war?'

'The only woman for most of it. Photographer, I mean. Some of her pictures . . .' He shook his head. 'She won a Pulitzer for her shot of dead soldiers in the morgue.'

'Wow.'

'And she took me on.' He exhaled an awed stream of smoke that tainted the iridescent air. 'She was dubious at first. Thought I was a playboy.' He shook his head, liberated, momentarily, from his sophisticated shell. 'I can't believe my luck.'

That day I found his awe bizarre. Later, when I knew her, I would recall my narrow-mindedness with shame. Simone had brought up her brothers after her parents died in a car crash, and was funding the education of three Bosnian men. But that day we had only one conversation. It was after lunch. She was sitting in a cut-down plastic chair by the pool reading a biography of Lee Miller, her face speckled like an egg in the shadow thrown by her torn straw hat.

'You met Gorbachev, didn't you?' she said. 'I'm dying to know. What's he like?'

'Oh, extraordinary. He has this incredible power. But a sense of humour too. A real depth.'

'Did you do the interview in London?'

'No, in Moscow. It was amazing.'

'You must love your work.'

'I do.'

'Do you travel a lot?'

'Not really. Sometimes to LA. Or New York.' I scratched my leg. 'You must find it strange being here, after Bosnia.'

She nodded. 'But you burn out. It's a weird place.'

'Especially for a woman.'

'Especially for a woman. Though huge camaraderie. We take care of each other.' She gave a wry shrug. 'Now we're into weddings and white lace.'

'*You're* not wearing lace?'

'No!' She grinned. 'I'm not so bothered about getting married. Jean wants to.'

'Well, it's nice.'

'It is nice.'

Our eyes met, and we smiled, and I felt a flash of pleasure. I sensed then that she knew more than I did – that she was further up the mountain. She and Jean-Pierre got married and began trying for a baby. But she didn't get pregnant, which devastated them both. By the time Patty came on the scene Simone was nearly forty, and had given up hope.

CHAPTER 4

On the Tuesday after we went to Sussex I came home to find a Crunchie Bar in the letterbox. A yellow Post-it was stuck to it: 'Lunch was wow. Please come Soho House 7pm Wenesday next week its my birthday. Patsy xxx.'

I was charmed and RSVP'd yes on a neon green Post-it. That night I met the rest of Patty's friends.

It was a February evening. The streetlamps were yellow on the black branches of the trees and flung wavering zigzags over the dark chasm of the river. In the club there was a musty smell of wet coats and cigarettes, but no Patty. I picked up a paper. Monicagate, it seemed, had ended: Clinton had got away scot-free.

Made a nationwide TV address from the White House Rose Garden. Red-eyed and voice trembling slightly, he said: 'I want to say again to the American people how profoundly sorry I am for what I said and did to trigger these events and for the great burden they have imposed on Congress and the American people . . .'

'Drink?'
'Gin and tonic, please.'

. . . saved by the court of public opinion. But his credibility is in tatters, his legacy forever tainted and he will go down in history as only the second president to suffer the ignominy of impeachment. 'He will be remembered as the most polished liar we have ever had in the White House,' said Republican Senator Robert Bennett.

I looked up. There was still no sign of Patty. But the two other people sitting stiffly by themselves were also waiting, I presumed, for our get together. One was a blonde with a lined, lived-in face that would have been pretty five years ago and dirty hair pinned untidily to her head. She was smoking and reading a book called *How To Manage Your Time*. The man had a jowly, arrogant face that melted into his neck and wore a large signet ring. He kept looking at the blonde. Finally he leaned over. 'Are you Queenie Holmes?'

She raised uninterested blue eyes. 'Yes.'

'I think we've met. You're a friend of Patty's.'

'So we have. You took that coke and never paid me.'

I heard a breathless giggle and Patty materialised

in the doorway. She was in an extraordinary outfit – a skin-tight white dress that strained at its straps like a greyhound. 'Baby, I'm so sorry,' she exclaimed breathlessly, manoeuvring up to the blonde. 'I got all made-up and my hair done and everything, and then I remembered I hadn't had a shower, and I had to start all over again. Then the washing-machine man arrived, and Ramzi called . . .'

She bent to kiss her, providing a startling view of her breasts.

'That's okay,' Queenie said calmly, offering her cheek. 'At least I'm not in that horrible hotel.'

'Oh, that was Ed,' Patty said. 'He went nuts whenever I went out.'

'He went nuts full stop.'

The jowly man slunk behind Patty. 'Good evening,' he said in a low voice, running a hand intimately down her back. 'How good of you to come.'

She jumped. 'I didn't think you'd get my note! I couldn't remember the address. I thought: "I'll send it anyhow" – and here you are! D'you like my dress? I got it specially. Joyce says it's indecent. But I made her get me into it, because soon I'll be old and have to live in slippers and kaftans. Logan, you know Queenie. And –' her breath, sweet with alcohol, fell over me '– this is Lottie. Tyrone couldn't make it. He said to say he was mortified.'

Logan's gaze snapped me like a camera, then raked Patty's dress. 'I like your dress very much.

Though frankly I'm amazed I'm here. "The house with the blue door opposite the pet shop." Not the most helpful description.'

'But you got here. Which is more than I thought I'd do. I feel so insecure! Thirty-two! Joyce made me swallow a whole glass of Milk of Magnesia. I thought I was going to throw up.'

'How is the old boot?'

Joyce was clearly not in favour with Patty's friends. When she appeared, in a purple trouser suit smelling of second hand shops, Logan and Queenie greeted her without enthusiasm and sat as far away from her as possible. As we got drinks two more guests arrived.

One was a bald ex-alcoholic called Anton Lord whom I knew slightly from university – he had been the year above me. The other was a small-faced man in a leather jacket that looked as if it belonged to his older brother and sunglasses that he took off to reveal a black eye going green and purple. 'You look well. Why?' was his cryptic greeting to Patty. 'I'm Tony,' he informed us. 'Sorry I'm late. There you go.' He tossed a box into Patty's lap. 'Don't use it at once.'

She grinned with delight. 'What is it? Tony's a really rich banker.'

'Humph!' Tony said, pleased. 'Go on. It won't bite.'

It was a pot of the new wonder cream, *Crème de la Mer*. 'Made by scientists,' Patty assured us. 'For burn victims.'

'Fashion victims, more like,' Tony muttered, but you could tell he was pleased.

The presents were instructive. Logan – who was, he informed me, her first director – gave her nothing. Queenie bought Patty a red plastic bracelet and a package in pink tissue paper that they giggled over and put away without revealing. Joyce, she informed us, had given her a hardback of *The Method* by Stanislavski. Anton gave her a copy of his first book.

There was no sign of Ramzi. Patty explained that he was 'coming, he just has some stuff to finish' – but nine o'clock came and went without him making an appearance. She didn't seem to care. She chattered gaily, the dress straining at the straps and her thighs, tipsy and happy and hopeful.

But by ten we were starving. 'Where is he?' Queenie muttered.

'He's probably forgotten,' observed the director.

'You've met him?'

'Last week.' He raised his eyebrows meaningfully.

'Not another one?'

'Without a doubt.'

We drank until 10.30pm. Joyce sucked a Gitane, holding the cigarette theatrically between her third and fourth finger. 'What happened to your eye?' she asked Tony.

'Don't ask. I got mugged by a pregnant woman.'

'How do you know she was pregnant?'

'She had a bloody great bump. Bloody cow took my phone.'

'Didn't you go after her?' asked Anton.

'Of course I did. Bloody tart got away.'

'Have *you* met him?' the director asked me.

'Who?'

'Lover boy. The new boyfriend.'

'No.'

'Think it's serious?'

'She seems to.'

'Does she?' He narrowed his eyes.

I yawned. 'So how come you directed Patty?'

'How do you mean?'

'You said you were her first director.'

'Oh. Yes. Well, we hired her to play a nurse. It was a fucking nightmare. Every time we went to shoot she was AWOL – sobbing in the canteen. It was after her marriage broke up. Then I watched the rushes.'

'She was married?'

'To some loser. I never met him.' He lit a cigarette. 'She was pure magic on screen. It was an alchemy. None of us had seen anything like it. I'm trying to get her to do something now.'

'Wow.'

We looked at Patty. She was clearly in the middle of a story: whisking her skirt, grinning, from side to side.

'I'll tell you her talent,' Logan went on. 'She sets up a challenge in every man. They don't know whether to smack her or take her to bed.'

Patty caught our eye. Smiling, she mouthed: 'What?'

'Of course, no education,' he mused. 'But that can be dealt with. It may even be the reason.'

'For what?'

'Her charm.' He stabbed out his cigarette. 'But she won't make it.'

'Why not?'

'Too self-destructive. That's the interest of it, too, of course – watching the struggle. Sometimes she wins. Mainly she don't.'

'I think that's incredibly –' I began angrily, but at that moment Tony plumped himself between us.

'So what's your connection?' he asked me.

I smothered another yawn. 'I'm a friend. We met in LA.'

'You live there?'

'No, I went for work.'

'Well, I'm a big fan of LA. I know a lot of people think it's got no culture. I don't agree.' He laced his hands trustfully behind his head. 'I met Patty in the Big Apple.'

'Oh, yes?'

'She was there for an audition. I was hiring for my company. We got chatting. She's quite a gal.'

'She certainly is.'

'I was with my mate Kevin in the East Village. She was dancing on a table. Literally dancing on a table. I said: "Send that girl some fizz." Five minutes later she came up. "I love champagne," she said. "It makes me feel like a fountain."' He

58

chuckled fondly. 'She gets through more than a fleet of maiden ships.'

'So you're a banker?'

'Was. I'm unfortunately going through a divorce. For twenty years I was in the City. September eighteenth, I handed in my notice. Same night my wife says she's leaving. I took my eye off the ball. I thought she'd wait. I was wrong.'

'I'm sorry.'

'Oh, it's amicable. So I'm single, with money to burn, ready to have fun. At Christmas I'm off to Cape Town. I'm looking for a girl to take with me. I did so much travelling while I was in the City I've been given two free first-class plane tickets anywhere in the world. Trouble is they expire next month.' He eyed Patty. 'It's hard to get a straight answer.'

'Well, it sounds great.'

'No, I was thinking of Patty. She'll come. I told her, "We'll have a ball. Just toss a bikini in a bag." I look after my girls. I gave my wife everything – trouble was, I didn't keep my eye on the ball.'

I went to the loo and stared dismally at my reflection. When I came back Ramzi had arrived.

He was middling tall, with a pigeon chest, blunt-toed shoes and unpleased black eyes that failed to keep their opinion of the gathering to themselves. He was good-looking, objectively, but there was something so seedy about him that he was quite literally repellent.

Patty was hanging off his arm. 'Lottie!' she cried.

59

'This is *Ramzi*. Ramzi, this is Lottie! Isn't he gorgeous?'

'How do you do?'

'Hey.'

'I'm so happy you're here!' Patty told him. 'We've been having such fun!'

That meal was infused with Patty's happiness. Because she was happy Ramzi was there – despite our dismay. She laughed and giggled and told stories and drank from his glass and stroked his leg and ran her hand through his hair. He fidgeted through it all, furtively checking his phone with curiously thin, pointed fingers. We exchanged perhaps three sentences. I said something like, 'It's nice to meet you – Patty's told me so much about you,' and he said: 'Yes?' and stared at me so suspiciously I thought he must have misheard. Then I asked what he was reading at the moment and he cleared his throat and said, '*FHM*.' That might have been a joke.

I was next to Anton Lord, who raised his small eyes to stare at him in disbelief. He then ate without bothering to speak, his gaze flicking up to check out each new arrival. Once he lifted a hand in a limp salute. The talk eddied round us. It was of dotcom launches and floats, get-rich-quick schemes and wild anecdotes of people who had made millions on the Internet. At last I said, 'So how is everything?'

'Er, fine. Have we met?'

'We were at Oxford together.'

'Were we?'

'Yes. At Magdalen.'

'I was at Magdalen.'

'I know. You were the year above me.'

'Really?' He chewed dubiously. 'What year?'

''86 to '89.'

'I was '85 to '89.'

'I know.'

We leaned back as a waiter filled our glasses. I said eventually: 'So you've written a book.'

'Two, actually. I've just finished my second.'

'A novel?'

'More of a memoir. Philosophy crossed with memoir.' He checked his Rolex. 'This is going on forever. How do you know Patty?'

'I met her in LA.'

'We met here. I used to take her picture.' He gave a thin smile. 'She's a prick tease.'

I disliked him immensely. 'I think she's great.'

The meal dragged on. From the street rose thin clamorous sounds of revelry. Across the table Ramzi's gaze was blank and inward. Queenie complained: 'And to add to my woes, I came in to find my landlady's son sniffing my knickers! I said, "What the fuck are you doing?" He said, "My mother has a spare key."'

'You weren't the one who did that magazine?' Lord asked. 'You're not Petronella?'

'No.'

'I thought not.' He licked his lips, looking at Ramzi. 'He's a nasty piece of work.'

61

'Why do you say that?'

'Well, he's a drug dealer. She's got the worst taste in men I've ever seen.'

I felt the onset of giggles. 'But she never slept with you?'

When I was in the loo for the third time Patty hurried in. A red wine stain splashed her front. But her eyes were like stars. 'Isn't he sexy?' she cried. 'Don't you just love him?'

'I haven't really talked to him.'

'Oh, you must. He's so lovely. I know he doesn't look it, but he's shy. I'm cross with Joyce. She hasn't talked to him once.' She lifted up her hair, vamped in the mirror a moment, and let it drop. 'At least he treats her like a human being. At least he gives her the benefit of the doubt.'

When the bill came Ramzi stared at it, fingered his cap and announced he had forgotten his wallet. Joyce paid for all three. Outside he nodded gravely at each of us and steered Patty into the night – presumably to catch a night bus home.

Joyce and I were left standing on the pavement.

'Well?' I asked.

She shook her head. 'My God. It is beyond words.'

CHAPTER 5

The next week I heard nothing from Patty. But fragments of that evening kept floating back to me – Anton Lord's lips mouthing 'She's a prick tease', the banker's leather cuffs, Ramzi's eyes, hard as a street child's in Delhi. Then I opened the front door to get the milk and fell on top of her.

'Well, you don't need to tread on me,' she said plaintively. 'Can I have some Weetabix?'

She had had a row with Joyce.

'She wants to know everything I do,' she complained. 'I came home last week and she was trying on my dress.'

'Don't you wear her stuff?'

'Not when I can't fit into it! And this morning I caught her reading my diary. I think she's nuts.'

'I'm sure she is.'

She scrubbed her eye. 'It's like she wants to *be* me. She's always asking about my sex life. She asked Ramzi if he liked my blow jobs.'

I burst out laughing. 'So move out.'

'I think I will. Can I move in with you?'

I stopped laughing. 'Oh, Patty, no.'

'Oh, please! We can hang out! We can watch videos. You can teach me to cook.'

'I can't cook.' I thought of her bedroom. 'I'm a bit of a neat freak.'

'I can be neat! I can be quiet! I won't even have people over. You won't even know I'm here!'

'I'm really not –'

'I *promise* I won't make a mess. And I can do stuff for you! Clean, and stuff! I'm a really good ironer!'

'I don't . . .'

But her bright face was impossible to resist. 'Well – okay. But just for a few days. Until you find something else.'

She engulfed me in a hug. 'I'm so happy! I'll be silent as a mouse.'

That night we got a video of a Sandra Bullock movie, *Hope Floats*, and ordered another Chinese. I told her things I had never told anyone, and she listened, sweetly, sympathetically, holding my hand. She seemed to have an infinite quality of acceptance, and the next day I felt strangely light.

That morning, Friday, I took her to Joyce's to get her things. We timed it for her 11 o'clock yoga class. But when we unlocked the door the flat had an occupied feel, and in the sitting room we found Joyce sitting on the sofa.

Patty jerked to a halt. 'Oh!'

Joyce stood, inserting a bookmark into a dense green paperback. 'Where on earth have you been? I've been awake half the night.'

Patty threw me a horrified glance. 'I've been staying with Lottie.'

'With Lottie? Why didn't you tell me?'

'Why should I?'

For a moment Joyce looked angry – then she walked over to Patty and put an arm around her shoulders. 'Well, it doesn't matter,' she said. 'Just call me next time. Come, dear, I've made some soup. You look worn out.'

'I don't want soup.'

'Then I'll put you to bed. I'll put the blanket on. You look absolutely done in.' She turned her restless gaze to me. 'Thank you, Lottie. We'll manage from here.'

But Patty moved from the circle of her arm. 'You don't seem to understand,' she said. 'I've come for my things.'

Joyce blinked. 'What?'

'I told you. I'm moving out. I'm going to live with Lottie. You're giving me the creeps.'

'What?'

'I don't like it! I don't like the way you act!'

Joyce had gone white: was staring as if she'd been hit. 'Is this some kind of joke?'

'No! I don't like you reading my diary. I don't like you treating me like a prisoner. I don't like how you are with Ramzi.'

'Silly child! Can't you see he's just using you? I'm trying to protect you!'

I went into the hall and shuffled uncomfortably in front of the bookcase. The contents were all of a kind. *The Zipless Fuck. A Life of Eva Braun. The Feminist's Guide to Spiritualism*. Their voices filtered thinly through the door.

'Do you think *she* cares about you? Do you think she's going to love you like I do?'

'I don't *want* you to love me!' Patty shouted. 'I want you, to teach me yoga!'

The voices rose and fell a minute longer. Then Patty ran past me into her bedroom. Joyce came out and stood in front of me. She had been crying: the wrinkles round her eyes had deepened. She looked devastated.

'I'm sorry,' I said, and I think I gave a rather pathetic smile.

She just stared. 'You won't win, you know.'

I laughed nervously. 'I didn't know it was a war.'

But she kept on staring. 'You'll come to your cakes and milk. She doesn't have anything to give. She's a child – she only loves herself. I mothered her for years. The minute I ask her to do one thing for me she wails she's being used.'

Patty burst from the bedroom. She was dragging two canvas bags, and I do remember thinking it was a bit odd: that she acted as if Joyce wasn't there – as if she didn't even exist. 'I'm ready!' she cried. 'I'm all packed up.'

Joyce fixed her ashy eyes on her face. 'Please,' she said in a grinding voice.

I felt mortified – awful for her. But Patty didn't turn her gaze. She was eager as a child who has heard the scrape of her mother's key after a long week away. 'This is going to be so much fun!' she cried, tugging her bags in small heaves towards the door. 'I've never shared with anyone my own age before. We can be like sisters.'

CHAPTER 6

The funny thing was that living with Patty was actually very nice. I had forgotten the pleasure of living with a human being – the animal warmth of company. And she was very sweet-natured. I suppose that was the key to the whole thing – her incredible charm.

So I began to look forward to coming home and felt hard done by on the nights when she wasn't there to welcome me. I began to hoard anecdotes from my day to make her face change and her mouth pucker into an 'O' of outrage or delight.

And she did make an effort. She did the washing-up every day, with concentration, like a child, and even used hot water when I told her that was what you did – she had the weirdest gaps in her knowledge. She left her dirty knickers on the bathroom floor only once or twice a week and even stopped losing her keys when I told her that next time I would send her back to Joyce.

And she really was sweet. She had a natural quality of joy – and rose to hope like a dolphin flying at the sun. It makes me sad now to think of the little offerings she would leave daily on my bed:

chocolate hearts wrapped in red foil, crumbling brownies from Mr Christian's, my horoscope, torn from some crappy magazine or other.

Those months I learned about her childhood. Though she never talked about her mother, she seemed to regard her father with warmth, even love. 'He was nice to me,' she said. 'Though he could be a bit naughty I didn't mind: at least he loved me.'

'How do you mean, naughty?'

'You know.' She smiled cloudlessly. 'Too close. He would bring me presents and he was never cross. He'd tell me stories about when he was little, growing up in Wyoming with six brothers and sisters – he used to walk barefoot to school.

'I was taken to see him,' she said, 'when he came out of jail. I was twelve, and my auntie came and drove me to his flat. She gave me a squashed fly biscuit and pushed me in the living room. He was sitting totally still, and his skin had gone white.

'I said to my Auntie, "What shall I say?" and she said, "Ask who he thinks will win the election." So I said, "Daddy, who's going to win the election?" He didn't say anything for ages and ages. Then he said, "I think Reagan."'

I didn't ask what had become of him – I had a sense of some unarticulated disgrace. Her real family, it was clear, were her entourage of help-meets: Joyce, before she was banished, Tyrone, a hairdresser with a nicotine face and whispery voice – they would dance all night in gay clubs, take

69

ecstasy, and pore over the lonely hearts together –
and her agent Johnny Ritter who, though crippled
by heart problems, worked for her devotedly. He
was in his sixties and had offered to marry her.
She turned him down: she was a dyed-in-the-wool
romantic.

And in those days she was in love with Ramzi.

Their relationship was wildly up and down.
Sometimes they would be all over each other and
she would be rapturous; other days they would
fall out and she would put herself to bed with a
plate of Marmite toast or moon tearfully round
the flat staring at her phone. As far as I could tell
he spent most of his time flirting with other
women or standing her up. Though, to be fair, she
was not well behaved herself. One week she had
dinners with five different men. When I remarked
that that was hardly conducive to a good relationship she stared at me in amazement: 'But
they're only friends!'

Those nights I could almost sympathise with
Ramzi, when, spit at the corner of his mouth, he
would scream at her before stalking to his BMW.
Then she would study her self-help books with
titles like *Are You The One For Me?* and weep herself
to sleep.

The reconciliations would come out of the blue.
I would unlock the door to find her whispering
happily on the phone, twirling hair round her
finger, one calloused yellow foot propped on top
of the other. She would while away enitre nights

experimenting with make-up and trying on dresses. Her absorption wasn't born of vanity, I eventually concluded: it was more as if she doubted she really existed. I once caught her stuffing tights into her bra. 'For God's sake!' I said. 'You don't need *more* padding!' She stared. 'But what else are people going to look at?'

Of course she was self-centred. She would ask the most embarrassing questions.

On sex: 'How much do you masturbate? I keep thinking I should practice but it's so hard to get going. I got myself a book but it didn't tell you how to come – and that's what I don't get. Or maybe I have and I didn't know. What exactly happens when you have an orgasm?'

Or: 'I don't think I have any friends. Some mornings I wake up and have no one to call. Is everyone like that, or just me?'

I came back one day to find her craning at her bum. 'What on earth are you doing?' I demanded. She twisted in surprise. 'Checking if I have a stain from my period.'

The downside was the phone calls. Men rang for her all the time. Or came round, smiling hopefully on the step: 'You know when she'll be back?' They were an extraordinary collection, English and French and American and Polish, all different ages and shapes, and I had no doubt she had met them in a bar, or one of Tyrone's clubs, or maybe even on the street.

But Logan was right about one thing: she was

talented. When she rehearsed her voice and her posture would change – it was an alchemy. She pondered 'characterisation' and 'motivation' and pored over the lives of stars. In between she would watch EastEnders and muse on her dreams, referring to me for elucidation. I always thought they were peculiarly childlike, as if she had been frozen by scientists at some early stage of development. She had a recurrent nightmare, for example, that she was being chased round a hut in the woods by a bear. In another she was trying to get cakes from her father. But Joyce kept blocking her way, goose-stepping like a Nazi.

In real life, of course, the situation was quite different: Joyce was desperate to make up. I came home one night to find her huddled on the step. She raised a ravaged face.

'She won't even see me!'

'I'm sure she will. She's just upset.'

But Patty wasn't rational on the subject. When I suggested she was being hard on her friend she gnawed her thumb so savagely it bled.

At the end of March I went to Courchevel with the copywriter. Patty, who couldn't ski, told me cheerfully she would spend the week with Ramzi.

I came home to find her in her bed, the duvet scattered in crumpled Kleenex like water lilies. She was shivering and looked half a stone thinner. Tears leaked from her eyes. I was shocked. 'Patty? What's happened?'

But she just shook her head and turned over in a weary, listless movement that stabbed my heart. I stared at her for a minute and then went to get some more tissues. There was only one explanation: Ramzi had dumped her; he had met someone else.

But she wouldn't tell me anything that day: whenever I tried to talk she would burst out crying. I made her some Marmite toast, drew her curtains and went downstairs. That evening the only sound from her room was of her sobbing in a long-drawn-out, forlorn way. But when I went upstairs the next morning I found her sitting up in bed staring at her hands. Her eyelids were pink and swollen as cod's roe.

'We broke up,' she said in a small voice.

'Oh, honey.'

'I'm so cold. I can't seem to get hot.'

'Do you want another duvet?'

She nodded pitifully.

'I'll get you one.'

I smoothed it on her and she met my eyes for the first time. 'He dumped me.'

'Oh, honey.'

'He said he never wants to see me again.'

'Oh, dear.'

'I don't think I can live without him.' She raised a blind, pleading face. 'Do you think I can call him?'

'Sweetie, is that a good idea?'

'But I want to!'

'I don't know, honey.'

She burst into tears.

'At least try to eat something,' I said. 'Do you want me to make you some toast?'

At which she started sobbing even harder.

It took her ages to get well. She went down with flu and then bronchitis and then started complaining that it hurt her to sit down – it turned out she had a cyst on her coccyx. I took her to casualty. When we got home there was a flush of colour in her cheeks, and I left her propped on two cushions with her favourite self-help book and a packet of Minstrels.

I put her flush down to illness. But when I came back from the supermarket I found her frantically applying mascara. She was in her best dress, a racy, lacy number, and her cheeks were hectic. 'I spoke to him! He's coming,' she breathed, and her face was so full of hope I found myself actually hoping that he would – that they would get back together if it would make her life possible.

Her nails were still wet when the phone rang.

'Oh,' she said, and put it down as if she had forgotten where she was.

He had rung to say he wasn't coming.

'He says he can't forgive me.'

'What the fuck does that mean?'

Which was when it came out that she had been sleeping with Johnny Ritter.

It took me a moment to take in.

'But why the fuck were you doing that?'

74

'I didn't *mean* to! I just felt sorry for him! I don't know what the big deal is!'

'You were going out with Ramzi!'

'But I didn't *love* him! It wasn't important!'

The facts themselves were simple enough. Johnny Ritter had come round and found her in a bath towel. Ramzi had caught them red-handed – it was at this point in the story I learned he had a key.

The one ray of light was Ramzi's disappearance. I never saw him again, and, though Patty mourned him for months, I don't think they ever spoke after that. He certainly never answered the phone when she called, and I know that she tried.

Looking back, I think it was then that my feelings for her began to alter. It was the first moment of doubt: the first stirrings of mud in the pond. Because I could understand her having terrible taste in men – I could just about understand her dating a drug dealer. But two-timing him with a man of sixty-five? It was gross. Yet hadn't she slept with Ritter out of pity? Was I the cold one?

I sighed in the chill kitchen, waiting for the kettle to boil. Outside it was windy and wet: the birch trees flailed and bucked as though they were being lashed. Talking about it later, I found myself describing her as a cuckoo in the nest, and I think in many ways that was what she was. Because she had no idea of deferral – because she took what she wanted, like a child.

CHAPTER 7

That April, as the breeze softened towards spring, and the cruise missiles flew East for Kosovo, I met Tyrone. He was the hairdresser, Patty's best friend, and judging from her artless anecdotes, the repository of her most urgent secrets.

But not all, I discovered, when I joined them for lunch at Patty's insistent invitation. The venue was a slick French restaurant called La Brasserie in South Ken; I found her perched beside a doll-sized man with parchment-yellow teeth and an ingratiating smile. A pair of large red sunglasses was propped on his bulbous head.

'There you are!' Patty exclaimed. She jumped up. 'This is Ty*rone*.'

He stuck out a skinny hand, looking at me from large eyes that had yellow flakes of sleep entwined in the lashes.

'How do you do?' I asked politely.

'Hello.'

His eyes swept my face so keenly that it made me wonder what he saw there. But he seemed pleasant enough. 'Oh!' he said. 'You're so little! I thought you'd be really huge.' His gaze focused behind me. 'Oh. My. God. I *want* one!'

A stout white-haired woman in a Barbour was leading a pair of toy poodles down the street. They had shiny black eyes and raw, painful-looking shin-bones. They trotted eagerly, sniffing the breeze.

'Oh, I love poodles!' Patty said.

Tyrone stared at them raptly. 'And they're easy to train. Poodles are the cleverest breeds. But they have diabolical breath. I couldn't have a dog with bad breath.'

'What can I get you?' asked the waiter.

'Ooh,' mused Tyrone. 'Hmm. Maybe a croque-monsieur.'

'That's with ham,' Patty said.

'I know darling.'

'I don't like that one.'

'So don't have it.'

'I shan't. I'm going to have cheese and onion soup.'

'We shall have one French onion soup. And a croque-monsieur.' Tyrone squinted at the menu. 'And a bottle of wine. Let's be naughty.' He looked at me enquiringly.

'I'm fine. I'll just have a latte.'

Patty stared. 'You're not going to eat?'

'I'm not really hungry.'

Tyrone turned to Patty. 'So. You're looking fabulous: I love the scarf. How's tricks?'

'Really good!'

'You've not heard from the greaseball?'

She shook her head.

'Thank goodness. I was having dire thoughts. Now then. I have a delicious man for you. A gorgeous film producer. Slight class A habit – but not too serious.'

'Oh, if it's coke I'm not interested,' Patty said. 'I don't mind a bit of a temper, but really, coke turns men into such shits.'

'*That's* what I was going to tell you,' Tyrone said. 'You'll never guess who I saw in Berlin.' He paused for effect. '*Erich.* An ex-boyfriend of ours,' he observed to me. 'When I say of ours, I am not joking. Pattybelle converted him.'

'Well, I didn't know he was gay! And he was superfab in bed.'

'Oh, please. I try not to be judgemental, but really, Erich was *not* superfab in bed.'

Patty's phone went. She picked it up.

'Oh,' she said. 'Hi.' She gave us a glance. 'No. I'm at lunch.'

Tyrone stared at me. 'Who's that?'

'God knows.'

'She got another boyfriend?'

'Not that I know of.'

'Did you absolutely loathe Ramzi?'

'Absolutely.'

'Those *mossy* teeth. I don't think he *ever* flossed.'

Patty was giggling down the phone. She bit her lip. 'Really. I can't.'

'Maybe it's the one she fancies,' Tyrone said. He sucked at his teeth. 'The married one.'

'Which one's that?'

But he was looking at Patty.

'Maybe,' Patty was saying in a pleased, childish voice. Her eyes slid consideringly to one side.

Tyrone gave her a hard stare and waved his hand in her face.

'I've got to go,' she told the phone. 'Yes. No. I don't know.'

She pressed the off button and pushed her hair brightly. 'Has our food come?'

'Who was that?' demanded Tyrone.

'What?'

'Pattybelle Bellani, who was that?'

The waiter came up. 'One croque-monsieur. One soup. Who's having soup?'

'I am,' Patty said. She awarded the waiter a ravishing smile. 'That looks scrummy. *Thank* you.'

'Don't think you can change the subject,' Tyrone told her. 'There are no secrets from me. This is not a day of secrets. Who was that on the phone?'

'No one,' Patty said. Her gaze hovered over the table. She selected a piece of bread. 'Gosh I'm hungry. I could eat a horse.'

'Was it Ramzi?'

'No!'

'The married man?'

Her eyes flickered. She shook her head.

'Not *Erich*?'

'No!' She rubbed her nose. 'It was Ed.'

'Ed Kaplan? From *America*?'

'Well of course from America,' Patty said. She

widened her eyes. Then looked at her nails. 'By the way, where *is* the Mandarin Oriental?'

The Mercedes with 'TOP GIN' plates had been waiting, engine purring, for twenty minutes. Patty hurried into the kitchen. She tore off a sheet of kitchen towel, crouched down and began stuffing it into the toes of her sling-back shoes. Tyrone watched with raised eyebrows. It was three hours after our lunch at La Brasserie and two hours before Mark and Christine, Simone and Jean-Pierre were due at mine for supper.

'I can't believe you're ditching me,' Tyrone said. 'You hated him. He fucked you over.'

'Well, I know. Well, he didn't. Well, he's sorry.'

'Is that honestly the best you can do?'

Patty shoved her feet in the shoes. 'We're just – having fun! Isn't that allowed any more?'

'Not with that tosser.' He grabbed her ankle. 'Have you forgotten what he did?'

She threw him a glance of warning. 'God! It's like being back at school.' She let out an irritated laugh. 'He just wants to have dinner!'

'You're in a river in Egypt.'

'I'm *not*! He *feels* bad! He wants to say *sorry*!' She wrenched her hair into an elastic band and reached for her coat.

'I didn't even know you were in touch,' I said.

'I'm not!'

'He's still married?'

The bell rang.

80

Patty snatched the top off her lipstick and frantically outlined her mouth in the blurry silver plate of the oven.

'Do you want me to get it?' I asked.

'Tell him to piss off,' advised Tyrone.

'No, don't!' Patty shrieked.

'Evening ma'am,' said Ed Kaplan.

Bulked on the doorstep, he seemed as if he had walked in from another planet. Everything about him, from the heavy folds of his face, the rich, tasteless raincoat, the blow-dried hair, and the lazy sexuality, marked his presence as foreign in that stucco English street.

He gave me a boyish grin. 'I'm sorry to trouble you. I was looking for Patty.'

Close to, he emanated an energy that made you more conscious of yourself; made the hairs lift and stand to attention on your arms.

'She's coming,' I said.

He ducked his head. 'A pretty night.'

'Yes, it's nice.'

We waited. As the silence became uncomfortable Tyrone came out of the kitchen. He folded his arms. 'She's not coming.'

Kaplan looked at him and took him in.

'No,' said Tyrone. 'She's not, and she doesn't want to see you again. She hasn't forgotten – if you have.'

Kaplan stared at him a moment. 'I haven't forgotten anything.'

Patty appeared. She stumbled a little on her

shoes. She looked at him pleadingly. 'I don't think I can come.'

'Why, are you sick?'

'Mm.' She avoided his eyes.

'Well, that's terrible.'

Kaplan stepped forward. Now he was half inside the door. It wasn't threatening – more like a chess master moving a bishop: strategic, a blocking move. He frowned. 'You do look a little pale.'

'I feel pale,' she said.

'But beautiful.'

He smiled at her and Patty gave an involuntary shiver, like a dog that has spied its master. Tears came to her eyes. 'Don't!' she said.

'She's *told* you,' Tyrone asseverated. 'So why don't you piss off?'

It was unfortunate that his voice was so much higher than Kaplan's, and his height so much smaller; the effect, unintentionally, was almost comic.

Kaplan switched his faded blue eyes to Patty. 'I took a suite,' he told her confidentially, as if only he and she existed. 'I got champagne and yellow roses. I wanted it to be a surprise. I wanted to see you. That's all. I just wanted to see you, and hear your voice.'

Patty swallowed.

'I just wanted to spend time with you, baby doll. Because I love you.'

She looked at him. She seemed to be trying to decide whether to believe him. I couldn't work out if he was spinning her a line – or if he really

82

meant it. He actually seemed genuine. 'I'm having kind of a hard time back there,' he told her in a quieter voice.

'Don't, Patty,' Tyrone warned.

Kaplan gave a twitch of irritation.

'It's been tough since you left,' he said. He put his hands in his pockets. 'You went just as things got really hot.'

'Don't fall for it!' Tyrone cried.

But Patty had stepped towards Kaplan. He put his arms around her and over her shoulder his eyes met ours. They had a glint of warning in them now, or triumph: a sort of absence of feeling. He continued to hold Patty to him as he led her to the car, working his keys from his pocket with one hand. She looked very small, very fragile, by his side.

'See you,' she called.

Behind them the gate slammed. The evening seemed suddenly empty, as if some essential energy had departed.

CHAPTER 8

That night, like the first, I worried about Patty. But I had guests, I was busy cooking food, and it didn't occur to me that the evening could have frightening proportions until right at the end. By then it was midnight and Jean-Pierre, Simone, Mark, Christine and I were up in the drawing room with our coffee.

The night, cool with nostalgic melancholy, breathed through the windows. A small moon hung yellow over the rooftops. The strains of a saxophone drifted from the council block behind. Everyone was softened, drunk, overfed; except Simone. All night she had been quiet and subdued. Now she sat apart from us by the window staring at the stars. As I watched she smothered a sigh and rubbed her temples. The shadows deepened the lines in her forehead and I thought she looked old.

We were talking about the Internet – inevitably: no one at the time discussed much else, apart from Clinton. Mark David, tall and spindly in front of the fireplace, was describing with wonder a dotcom launch party he had been to the previous night.

'I think it's incredible,' Jean-Pierre said. 'It's a revolution. I want to be part of it.'

'You do?' Mark stared at him. 'I doubt it will last.'

'Exactly!' Christine agreed.

'I think it might,' said Jean-Pierre. 'A friend of mine said yesterday I could join his company. He's launching a gambling site. He's hoping to float in December.'

From the window, Simone stirred. 'But you're a writer.'

He shrugged with a hint of bitterness. 'I'm a failure.'

'You're not!'

'Gambling could be interesting,' Mark said. He leaned against the mantelpiece. 'It lends itself to the Internet, certainly.'

'Everything lends itself to the Internet. According to George. People'll be buying books and CDs soon – even clothes.'

'They're not going to buy *clothes* on the Internet!' cried Christine. 'There's no way they'll buy *clothes*!'

'They already are.'

'But that's ridiculous! How do they know if they'll fit?'

'So, will you do it?' Mark asked.

Jean-Pierre pushed away his coffee cup. 'Maybe.' He gave a faint shrug. 'Seize the day.'

Mark raised his eyebrows. 'Is that a good philosophy?'

'It's certainly Patty's.' I said. I got up, smiling. 'Who's for more coffee?'

Mark took his arm from the mantelpiece. 'This is your friend?'

I nodded. 'She only acts on impulse.'

'She's a funny girl,' Christine observed musingly. She touched her spotty jaw-line with the tips of her fingers. 'Where does she come from anyway?'

'LA,' Jean-Pierre said.

'She's with her LA ex-boyfriend as we speak,' I said. 'For her sins. Ed Kaplan, so called.'

'Ed Kaplan?' Mark frowned. 'I know that name.'

'He's a property developer, I think. From America.'

'Kaplan.' His stare sharpened. 'Not the Democrat fundraiser?'

'I've no idea.'

'He's very bad news. He was linked to the call-girl scandal.'

'That's right,' Jean-Pierre said. He leaned forward, remembering. 'The Smoking Gun scandal.'

I put down the coffee pot. 'You're not saying he *killed* a call-girl?'

'No, no. But there was some scandal. I believe he was sleeping with her.'

'*Anyway*,' said Christine. 'I love your mirror. Is it French?'

'He sounds bad news,' Simone said.

I nodded. 'We tried to stop her. But she wouldn't be told. He is – very charismatic.'

'He's a crook,' Jean-Pierre said.

'Ooh,' said Christine. She gave a pleasurable shiver. 'Marky, we should make a move.'

Just then the front door opened and we heard footsteps hurry up the stairs. Patty came past the doorway. She was bundled in a loose-fitting yellow coat. A red scarf covered her hair. She stopped in confusion at the sight of so many people. 'Oh!' she said. 'Hello.'

I stood up. 'Patty! Are you okay?'

'Yes, fine!' she cried. She looked at us, nervously touching her tongue to her lip.

'Are you really?' I insisted. 'I was worried. Where did you go?'

'Oh,' Patty said. She seemed to be trying to gather herself. 'Well. We had such a good time. We played pool.'

'At the Mandarin Oriental?'

'No. Um, a bar.'

She was holding her hand in her coat. Her face was pale. I thought she looked as if something had frightened her.

'So it was fine?' I confirmed.

'Oh, we had such fun,' Patty said. 'We went to Nobu and ate these tiny shrimp parcels. We had a cocktail in a ballroom on Park Lane.' She smiled at Jean-Pierre. 'But I'm interrupting.'

Mark David sprang forward. 'Not at all! Please – sit down.'

'Thank you,' Patty said, and came hesitantly forward. A bar tang of cigarettes and spirits emanated from her, not unpleasant: a reminder of the busy, foreign world outside. 'Just for a moment,' she said. She perched carefully on the sofa beside Jean-Pierre, eyes down. 'It's such a lovely night,' she sang, and now I was certain something was wrong. 'It's like the moon's casting a spell on everything; like the pavements are plated in silver.' She looked at Jean-Pierre and away. 'We played pool with some bricklayers who told us about leprechauns.'

'Leprechauns?' Mark asked. He smiled.

Patty nodded, looking happier. 'Yes, from the Glen of Cloongallon. There's an oak tree that's six hundred years old where they live. They're guarded by a tree spirit.'

'The leprechauns?'

'Yes. It's the most beautiful place in the world, they said: I could visit any time.'

She blushed as if a thought had occurred to her and looked at the floor.

'And so you played pool?' Simone prompted kindly.

Patty looked at her with big eyes. 'I tried to. I wasn't very good.'

'Oh, I'm terrible.'

But Patty brought her thumb up to her mouth. Her eyes had gone went back to Jean-Pierre. But he was looking into the distance – a heavy, brooding stare.

Mark cleared his throat. 'Lottie was saying you were with Ed Kaplan.'

Patty blinked. 'Do you know him?'

'No. No, no.'

'Oh,' she said, and an indefinable look came over

her face, of sadness twinned with – weariness? Disillusion? She stood, still cradling her hand. 'I ought to go to bed.'

'What's wrong with your hand?' I asked.

'Nothing.'

'Let's have a look.'

'It's fine.'

'Let's see!'

She brought it reluctantly from her coat. The thumb was black and swollen to twice the size.

'Patty!'

But she pressed her lips together – it was not something she wanted to discuss. 'Well, good night.'

As the door closed we exchanged looks.

'Oh dear,' Simone said.

I put my hand on my throat. 'Do you think he hit her?'

'Not our business,' Jean-Pierre said. 'Come on, Sim. Time for bed. Long drive home. Don't let me forget my phone.'

'I hope she's okay,' Simone murmured.

Christine got to her feet, examining her finger-nails with a distant appreciation. 'I didn't think that yellow coat looked awfully good,' she remarked, tenderly touching her spots. 'It made her skin look all pukey.'

The next morning I found Patty staring out of the French windows with a sombre expression I had never seen before.

But when she saw me she jumped up and started smiling. 'I just saw a squirrel,' she said. 'Don't they run fast? With that funny tail whisking up and down. Do you think he'd eat bread if I put some out?' She came and leaned beside me as I put on the toast.

'I should think he'd prefer nuts.'

'I don't have any.' She put her chin in her hand and the sombre expression crept back. 'I wish I did. There's something so safe about nuts. I could bury them wherever I went and then they'd be waiting – I could dig them up whenever I needed them.'

'What's the matter?'

'Nothing!'

'How's your thumb?'

'It's fine.'

'Show me.'

She had bandaged it clumsily. The knuckle was yellow and black. 'Are you sure it's not broken?'

'I don't know.'

'I think it might be. Does it hurt?'

She shook her head.

'You should get it looked at.'

'I can't. I've got a modelling job.'

'Well, go afterwards.'

'Maybe.' She folded back the bandage. 'Did you have fun last night?'

'Yes, it was nice. Except for Christine.'

'I like her boyfriend.'

'He seemed to like you. Tea?'

'Please.'

She curled at the table and put her chin back on her hand. Once again that sombre look was on her face. She shook her head as if to physically be rid of it. 'So it was fun last night,' she said. 'Ed really spoiled me.'

'Except for your thumb.'

'That wasn't him!'

'I certainly hope not.'

She jumped. 'What's that?'

'What's what?'

'I don't know. Like a buzzing.'

We tracked the source to a mobile phone vibrating under yesterday's *Times*.

'Jean-Pierre's,' I said. I shook my head, smiling. 'He said he'd forget it.'

Patty reached for it. 'Did he leave it?'

'Last night. I'll call him.'

But before I could the doorbell rang. On the step, like telepathy, was Jean-Pierre.

'Morning,' he said. He had dark circles under his eyes. 'Hope I didn't get you up.'

'Not at all,' I exclaimed. 'Come in. We just found your phone.'

'Thanks.' He located it in Patty's hand; met her eyes; took it. He gripped it, not looking at us. 'Great. Thanks.'

'Have some tea,' I said. 'I've just made a pot.'

'No. Thanks. I've got to run.'

'Are you sure?'

'Yes.' He seemed incredibly uncomfortable. 'But thanks. It was fun last night.'

'Well, if you can wait one second,' I said, laughing, 'I'll give you that book I was telling you about.'

'No, I should –'

'It's just upstairs.' I poured him some tea. 'Patty will you give JP milk? I won't be a second.'

The book was by Elio Vittorini and I really wanted him to read it. It had an incredible scene with a poor man urging his wife to eat an orange on a ferry. But it took me a while to track down. I finally ran it to earth in the bookshelf outside the top bathroom.

'It's got this wonderful scene,' I said, opening the door to the kitchen. 'Where the guy's –'

I don't know what it was about them that startled me. I think it was because something had so clearly happened. Jean-Pierre was standing as far away from Patty as possible, right by the end of the kitchen counter. She was quivering like a moth at the table. She looked – hurt, is the only word I can use. He looked pissed off. They both stared at me when I came in, and I remember I gave an awkward laugh. 'Everything okay?' I said.

'Of course,' Jean-Pierre said. He took the book. 'Thanks,' he said. 'And thanks for last night.'

'Pleasure.' His discomfort baffled me. 'Well. Bye.'

I watched him walk down the path and looked at Patty. 'What was all *that* about?'

But she had her head down and her hair across her face. 'I have to go,' she said in a small voice, and went upstairs.

CHAPTER 9

Rain drilled the pavements that May bank holiday, the temperature plummeted, and bleak winter seemed to permeate the planet. I had had another row with the copywriter, and so instead of going on the nostalgic trip we had booked to Marrakech I stayed miserably at home. As I watched my phone for his texts (he sent two: vague, tantalising) I had increasing trouble getting up in the morning. Heaviness weighted my heart like concrete, and all life seemed pointless. I began to develop an allergy to the house when it was empty – the very shadows, the unchanging layout of the furniture, the cries of the children from the house next door, the smell as I unlocked the door. Even the news was depressing. Clinton was claiming Starr's impeachment proceedings were politically motivated: in a TV interview he informed the CBS anchor Dan Rather he felt stronger than ever. 'I do not regard this impeachment vote as some great badge of shame,' he told him. 'What has occurred here over the last four or five years was horribly wrong.'

When I went downstairs to make toast I

discovered the bread was mouldy and burst into tears. Then, walking through the rain to Westbourne Grove, I bumped into Mark David. In fact, he caught me physically by the arm.

'Oh, hi!' I exclaimed. I stepped back. 'Sorry, I didn't see you.'

'That's all right.' He looked at me penetratingly, and then swung from a savage gust of rain. 'What dreadful weather! Global warming, I suppose.' His face was slicked wet and cold.

'What are you doing here?'

'Trying to get Christine a present. We were due to go away but – work called.'

'What are you getting?'

'I thought perhaps jewellery.'

'A bracelet?'

'Or pearls.' He smiled thinly and we stepped out of the way of the churning wheels of the bus. I thought Christine was the only woman in London who would still want pearls for her birthday. 'Wow, pearls are hard,' I said. 'Normally you'd get them in the West End. Or Piccadilly. Maybe Sloane Street.'

Mark's hair lifted in thin tufts. 'Ah.'

'But there's Dinny Hall on Westbourne Grove. Or you could get her something to wear.'

'That's true.'

'Do you need a hand?'

'No. No, I don't want to trouble you.'

'Really, it would be a pleasure. I've got nothing to do. I've been absolutely miserable.'

'You're not with the copywriter?'

'We had a row.'

'Ah.'

We struggled up the street under his umbrella. But in Dinny Hall it became obvious that he hated anything modern, and as we stood in the rain trying to decide where else to try the whole thing became an exercise in awkwardness. We finally went to Agnes B. He was buying a red cashmere roll-neck that we had compromised on when I caught sight of Patty. By then it was bucketing down – she was being blown along the street like a Tesco bag. As I watched her umbrella snapped inside out. Her expression was priceless: a mixture of amazement and alarm. I burst out laughing, and Mark David looked at me in surprise.

'Patty,' I said, pointing. 'What is she like.'

I pulled open the door. Her dress was plastered wetly to her thighs and her hair was in dark rats' tails. But her face was dazzling. 'My God!' she cried, 'this *weather*! I feel like a *bathtub*.'

I grinned. 'Well, come in. At least it's dry.'

'Well, that's something,' Patty said. She came in and wiped her face on her sleeve. 'Oh, I'm really sorry, I took your umbrella. It was so wet, you see, and I was in such a rush –'

'It's fine,' I said, cutting her off – I had developed a strategy with Patty, which was to take her things as ruthlessly as she took mine: she never seemed to notice. 'You remember Mark David.'

'Oh, hi!' she exclaimed. She wiped her nose and

I swear her expression, looking at him, wasn't particularly attentive. 'I just love this shop. I come in sometimes and just stroke the jumpers.' She laid her cold damp hands on the one we were buying. 'Oh, gosh! What a lovely jersey! I always wanted a jersey like that: I think I'd feel so classy. Is it for you?'

The question was for me; I explained it was for Mark David – or rather, he corrected stiffly, his girlfriend. Patty smiled in awe. 'That's so *nice*. I wish *my* husband would have bought me red jerseys. It's beautiful. I think any girl would feel like a million dollars wearing this.'

Mark stared as if he had indigestion. 'You're married?'

She shook her head. 'I used to be. I wish I was. But it's so hard to get married. I thought it would be easy, but you look and you look and nothing ever seems to change.'

'You seem too young to have been married.'

'Well, I was twenty-one. He was Mexican – Jeez, we used to fight.'

'It's letting up,' I said.

We looked at the window. The rain had given way to an arrhythmic, unconvincing drizzle; a leaf drifted diagonally to join a dirty white plastic bottle on the bus stop roof; grey seemed to permeate the planet.

'There you go,' said the shop assistant. 'Hope she likes it!'

I buttoned my coat. 'Well. It was lovely –'

'Can I take you to tea?' Mark said suddenly, looking from me to Patty. 'As a thank you? Would you like a cup of tea?'

There was something poignant about the invitation, and I stared at him in surprise. Mark looked at Patty. 'Or – perhaps you'd prefer a glass of fizz?'

She shrugged. 'Well. Sure,' she said. She grinned at me and I grinned back and we went out into the rain, laughing, now, under our umbrellas.

At Café 206 a good-looking Italian waiter, leaning on the counter, greeted Patty with pleasure. 'That's Giovanelli,' she confided as Mark pulled out her chair. 'He's getting a divorce.'

'How do you know?'

'He told me. He wants to open a casino.'

'Why does he want to do that?'

'He likes poker.' She smiled. 'He's going to teach me.'

'I bet he is.'

'He's very good!'

She smiled up at him as he took our order. He flourished his little pad and went away kissing his fingers. 'Tomorrow!' he reminded her lasciviously.

Mark fingered his glass. 'Do you come here much?'

'Not really,' Patty said. 'Sometimes. It's a good place to read scripts. Or, if I'm down after an audition, Giovanelli or Gianluca cheer me up. They give me free cakes. And I like to look out of the window and watch everyone go by; it makes me feel more cheerful.'

'And you're an old friend of Lottie's?'

'No, a new one,' Patty said. She smiled radiantly as Giovanelli poured the champagne, pushing back her wet strands of hair. 'We met in LA. It was such a funny day. I was really miserable – I was breaking up with my boyfriend.'

'I'm sorry to hear that.'

'Ed Kaplan,' I said.

'Ah.'

'Yes, Ed,' agreed Patty. 'And we had lunch by the pool, in Beverly Hills, and just totally hit it off. You know how you really get along with some people and you can't think of a thing to say to other ones? It was like that with Lottie. She could see I was in a state; she kept saying I should leave Ed, because he was married.'

'I don't think I *told* you to.'

'No,' Patty said. She frowned suddenly; brought her glass uncertainly up to her mouth.

Mark took a cautious sip from his own. 'But you're not American?'

'No, English. My dad was. American. I just went to live there. But it's so hard if you're an actress. And the directors are cunts. So I came back. England's much nicer. Everyone's so friendly.'

Mark adjusted his glasses. 'And you live with Lottie?'

'Yes. Because I fell out with my friend Joyce,' Patty said. 'She got a crush on me. She kept trying on my panties.'

'We'll spare Mark the details,' I said, but Patty

didn't seem to hear. 'She kept reading my diary,' she explained. 'Don't you think that's terrible? Diaries are sacred. My father always used to say "honour among thieves", and God knows he should know. I mean, I'm not saying I'm perfect, but I'd *never* read someone's diary.'

She waved to Giovanelli as he went out of the door. 'So I moved out. But it's been a blessing in disguise, really, because Lottie's so lovely. Are you two really close?'

'Well, we were at university together.'

'Gosh, so you're clever as well.'

'I don't know about that.'

'I bet you are. I bet you're a banker.'

'Far from it. I'm a writer.'

'A writer! What have you written?'

He told her, and she goggled. 'But they're amazing! I love those books.'

Mark David gave a doubtful smile. 'You're too kind.'

'No, really! I *loved* Allie Smith. I cried buckets when she died. I even dressed like her after I read that book – flowery hats I got from a second-hand shop.' She propped her chin on her hand, wide-eyed with wonder. 'So what are you doing now?'

'A play. *The Shoe Shine Boy.* You must come and see it.'

'I'd like to.' She put her little bitten hand on his arm – he stiffened, and I stared, but she just wanted to see his watch. 'Shit!'

'What?'

'I'm meeting Tyrone. I'm late. And I don't have any money.'

'She's under the delusion she's the Queen,' I observed drily.

Patty looked up from her bag. 'Who?'

'The Queen. Elizabeth. Our great sovereign?'

'What's she got to do with it?'

'She never carries money either.'

'Well, I do *normally*. I just had to buy so many things. Tampax, and deodorant, and a tooth-brush . . .'

'What is it with you and toothbrushes? You're like a vampire.'

'They're my teeth. I have to take care of them!'

She took the ten-pound note I was holding out. 'So how does she pay for anything?'

'Who?'

'The Queen.'

'Like you. Using her minions. Prince Philip.'

'Oh, I like him. He looks like he has a nice prick.'

She smiled at Mark. 'I hope your girlfriend likes her jumper.'

'Thank you.' His blush joined mine.

We watched her run through the door and almost collide with a bus as pigeons veered wildly out of her path.

I was mortified. 'Just ignore her,' I said. 'I'm sorry. She's been in LA.'

He moved his glass forward an inch. 'I didn't catch her surname.'

'Belle. With an "e".'

'How old is she?'

'Thirty-two.'

He didn't reply to that and I thought he was horrified by her, and by me, for knowing her, and I was very sorry to have introduced them.

But two days later I got a call from his secretary. A day after that two thick white envelopes arrived in the post. One was addressed to Patty, and one was to me. They were invitations to the press night of his play.

CHAPTER 10

Patty was so open about everything that I only realised she had drawn an invisible line around the subject of her mother when it was broached – in an unexpectedly dramatic way. One June morning a fortnight before Mark David's première, the phone rang and a man's voice asked for Mrs Bellani.

'You mean Patty?'

She was crouched on the back step reading *Hello!* and painting her toenails. It was a sunny day with a damp seaside edge to the air.

'For you,' I said.

She put the brush carefully back in its pot. 'Did you know Britney Spears had had a boob job?' she asked. She did a little dance, holding her breasts and singing in a throaty voice: '"Oops! . . . I did it again/ I played with your heart, got lost in the game/ Oh baby, baby/ Oops! . . . You think I'm in love/ That I'm sent from above/ I'm not that innocent."'

'*Phone*, Britney.'

She picked up the receiver and her smile went. She swallowed. Then nodded, as if whoever was on the other end could see her.

When she turned her face was pale.

'What is it?'

'My mum.'

'Your mum?'

'She's dying.'

'Oh God.'

She bit viciously at her finger. A fly zoomed from the window and flung itself back with a bang. I said: 'Where is she?'

There was a pause. She said: 'In Sevenoaks.' Then she turned and went into the garden.

I hesitated. Then I went and stood behind her. Her head was buried in her hands – I couldn't see if she was crying. 'Do you – want to go and see her?'

Her head shook.

'No?'

'No!'

I bit my lip. 'Perhaps you should, babe. You might never see her again.'

Her head shook.

'I could drive you. It might be good. It might be cathartic.'

'It won't be.'

'How do you know?'

'You don't under*stand.*'

'Understand what?'

She lifted a wet face. 'That she's so mean to me! She never says anything nice! Then I can't get her voice out of my head!'

'I'm sure she's not that bad! Think how you'll feel if you don't go, and she dies.'

'I don't *want* to.'

'But I think you should.'

She let out a sob.

'Really. I'm sure it'll be okay.'

Looking back I am amazed by my certainty – I would never have it now. But those days I saw life in black and white. And – I hadn't met her mother. But I had to admit there was something grim, on that burstingly beautiful June morning, about driving towards death. The cow parsley was exploding, lace-white, juicy with vigour, in the verges; the trees were muscular with green leaves and the fields rape-yellow, honey hanging in the air – everything was so fresh, and lovely, and alive.

Except Patty. I couldn't get anything out of her all the way down, except once, when she asked me to stop at a petrol station so she could go to the loo. I hadn't the courage to ask her how she was feeling, or to help with the map-reading, and we got lost twice before two hours later we pulled up outside the weather-beaten hoard that announced: 'Sevenoaks Senior Living'. The place was an ugly redbrick Edwardian villa set behind a cherry tree.

'Okay?' I said.

She nodded.

Inside it smelled of cleaning fluid. Red carpets covered the floors. Flat overhead lights threw a hollow orange glow over the buttoned green leather sofas and gilt-framed pictures, which seemed to be glued to the walls.

The girl at reception had nine silver rings on her fingers. 'What's the name?' she asked. She picked up a phone. 'Yes? Yes, I did . . . Well, that's not *my* problem.'

She looked at the computer and back with a different expression. She picked up a phone. 'I'll just get someone.'

Patty was staring at the floor. I wondered how her mother came to be there in the first place. How long had she been there? Who was paying for it all? Surely not the conman? Patty, perhaps? A different aspect of her unfolded.

'You've not been here before?' I asked.

She shook her head. She had a red spot on her chin and I felt a sudden sting of doubt. Perhaps I shouldn't have made her come. Her strange silence around the subject of her mother . . . I looked at her again. Her sundress had carved red dents on her shoulders. Her thumb was bleeding, the blood welling between the tiny sore shards of flesh.

A middle-aged man wearing a gold necklace came up to us. 'Mrs Bellani? I'm Steve. Your mother's carer.' He had bright blue eyes and thinning hair. His expression was kind – not the one men usually wore when they addressed Patty. She seemed to feel this, because she clasped her hands in an involuntary gesture and fixed her eyes on him.

'Now, I have some news,' Steve said. He cupped her arm. 'Your mother's still with us, but she's not here at the home. She had some breathing difficulties last night, and we had to send her to hospital. We did try to contact you to let you know. Perhaps you'd already left. But the hospital's very close, and you can go straightaway and visit.'

'Oh,' Patty said. She shivered.

'It's in Sidcup. She's getting the best care . . . Would you like to sit down?'

Patty nodded.

He walked her to the sofa by the fireplace. 'I can give you a map that shows you how to get there . . . Did you come by train?'

'No, drove,' I said.

'Ah, well, that's easy then. I'll write down the address. Do you know the area?'

With a look at Patty, he gave the scrap of paper with scribbled directions to me.

'She'll be pleased to see you, I'm sure,' he said. 'Obviously she is in some pain.' He sniffed and pulled out a yellow handkerchief. 'Sorry. Hay fever. The name's Steve Murray. I'll write it down. She'll be very pleased to see you.'

His words hung in the air as I worked my way round more unfamiliar roundabouts and red-brick industrial parks; Patty stared at the windscreen with fathomless eyes. I put my hand on her arm when we came to a stop in the hospital car park. 'You okay?'

She nodded.

'I just have to get a parking ticket.'

I put the ticket on the windscreen and she got out of the car, wincing a little when the door swung and hit her hip.

The electric doors of the foyer opened to reveal a drab café emitting smells of pizza, a small shop selling deodorant and newspapers with two elderly women frowning at the till, and a river of glossy linoleum. We set off along it behind two parents carrying a baby wrapped in a pink crocheted blanket and an old man pulling a wheelchair with his wife huddled in it, looking dimly to one side. The sun fell in yellow squares on the moles on her face. At the sign for the loo Patty stopped. 'I have to go.'

'Of course! No rush.'

A cleaner with a mop followed her through the door. I looked out of the window, feeling the warmth on my face. An ugly cluster of prefabs and a green playing field spread away into the distance. Two small figures walked on it kicking a ball back and forth.

'Okay,' Patty said. She had put on red lipstick and done something to her spot: it blared, vivid and angry.

She began walking. I followed her. Now she seemed more determined; as if something had hardened in her. I felt almost wrong-footed. It struck me that she was showing a new courage; I thought if it was me I would fall apart. We turned the corner.

Ahead shone another expanse of corridor. An

old lady inched past us in bed slippers, pushing a metal stand holding a bottle of liquid. At the double doors a sign ordered us to wash our hands with disinfectant.

'Oh, Mrs Bellani? Yes! She's just in here,' said the big-faced, bleached-blonde nurse on the reception desk. She got up, pulling her ponytail more tightly. 'Are you a relation?'

'Her daughter,' Patty whispered.

'Oh, that'll perk her up! She's a little bit brighter today, actually. Or she was this morning when I gave her her pills.'

'What is . . . what's she got?' Patty asked.

'Oh, you . . .' With a different expression the nurse came round to her, pulling from a box a preparatory tissue. 'It's cancer, I'm afraid.'

Patty looked at her. 'Of the bone marrow. Ewing's sarcoma, they call it. Not very nice.'

Patty brought her thumb to her mouth. 'Will she get better?'

'You'd need to ask the consultant. But we're very hopeful. They're very good here. You've not visited before?'

Patty shook her head.

'Well, she'll be ever so pleased to see you. Are you ready?' With a steadying touch she looked at her. 'Shall I take you through?'

By a coffee machine she pointed. 'That bed there. Just call if you need me.'

'I'll wait here,' I told Patty.

She clutched my sleeve. 'No!'

109

'I can't –' I saw the expression in her eyes. 'Okay.'

She began walking towards the bed. I couldn't see anything at first – the curtains were pulled round it. Then she disappeared between them and I followed.

Her tension had so infected me I was amazed to find myself looking at a perfectly normal-looking old lady. She was propped uncomfortably high on a mound of pillows, her head falling backward and a little sideways, a drip running into a soft, big-jointed freckled hand. It lay, curled upward, on the blue woollen bedcover. Her breath scraped in her chest, fluttering the white edge of the sheet. Her face was putty-coloured. A grey cardboard bowl stood on the window by a large black handbag, blocking the view of a small, cracked tarmac car park.

Patty came to a stop a foot from the bed. 'Mum?'

The hand twitched. The head turned. Her eyes were cloudy and heavy, as if drugged; a hand inched its way to the table. It grasped a pair of glasses and began the slow journey towards her head.

Behind the thick smeared lenses, the eyes fixed on Patty. 'Who are you?' she demanded in a high, cracked voice. She took a hoarse breath.

'Mummy,' said Patty. She reached and touched the small ridge of her leg. 'It's me.'

The woman gave a little shriek. She recoiled, and her head plunged crazily on the pillow.

'It's your *daughter*,' I said. '*Patty*.'

The old lady peered up, her wet bulbous mouth pushing in and out. She looked at Patty.

There was a pause. Patty was twisting her fingers. Her eyes were full of fear. The old lady seemed to recognise this, because she waited a moment, wet lips working. Then she took a breath and whispered: 'Not *my* daughter.' She smiled and theatrically inched her hand up to her lips, as if flicking away a crumb. Then, suddenly, she began tossing, heaving pitiful moans, exposing her wrinkled bosom inside her nightgown.

Patty put a terrified hand to my arm. 'What's happened?'

'I don't know!'

Patty hesitated, and then took her mother's hand. 'It's okay,' she whispered.

The old lady bolted upright and vomited black coffee-like grounds on the bed. Her breath seemed to have become wrenching efforts to live.

I threw down my bag. 'I'll get someone!'

The curtain parted and the blonde nurse came in. 'Now, Connie, what's all this?' she asked. 'Oh, dear. Bit breathy? We'll put on the mask. There. Now you'll be a bit more comfortable.'

As she adjusted the mask the old lady took wrenching breaths.

Patty turned wildly to the nurse. 'Is she all right?'

'Just a bit of a turn. Perhaps if you –'

She drew us through the curtains, and then went back in, followed by another nurse, a dark girl with a bob. We heard them murmuring to

111

Mrs Bellani while the remaining occupants of the ward occupied themselves as they had done, perhaps, for weeks. A large family were sitting round the bed of a grey-haired woman in a nightcap; she seemed to be dictating some kind of letter. At another bed a man and wife sat staring in silence.

The blonde nurse came out. 'She's fine,' she said reassuringly. 'We'll get the registrar to look at her this afternoon.'

Patty gave a panicky sob. 'She's not dead?'

'No, heavens, no!' She put her arm around her. 'Not nice, is it? Would you like a cup of tea?'

'She hates me,' Patty said.

'Oh, no, she doesn't! Here. Come to the day room. You can have a nice cup of tea. Well, as nice as we can make it. It's from a machine. I know it's hard. We see it every day, so we're used to it . . .'

With a comforting stream of chatter she settled us in a room dotted with cheap crumpled TV magazines and plastic chairs. Patty wiped tears from her eyes. In that place of sickness she seemed as out of place as a centrefold sprung to life. 'You mustn't take what she said to heart,' I said. 'She's obviously sick.'

She wiped her nose with her hand. 'She's never liked me.'

'She's just ill. She doesn't know what she's saying.'

'She hated me because of dad,' Patty said.

'Oh, Patty.'

The sun went in and we sat a moment in silence. 'I'll get us some more tea,' I said at last.

We drank it and put down our cups. The brown-haired nurse came back. 'Hi,' she said. 'I came to see how you were getting on.'

Patty sniffed. 'I don't know.'

'Hard, isn't it?' She crouched beside Patty. 'When it's your mum it's really hard. But she isn't in pain. She's being very well looked after. We're all doing our best for her.'

'Is she going to die?' Patty asked in a high voice.

The nurse put her arm around her. 'Well, she's not well. But we all have high hopes.'

'But she might die?'

The nurse hesitated. 'You'd have to ask the consultant. But she's doing as well as can be expected. She's a fighter, your mum.'

Patty let out a ragged sigh. She stood up.

'Where are you going?' I demanded.

Patty walked down the ward. She hesitated at the curtains, then went through. I looked away – it didn't seem right to watch. It was half an hour before she came back. Her face was pale and different somehow; there was something deeper in her eyes.

'Are you okay?' I asked.

She nodded.

I put back the magazine I had been reading. That afternoon something seemed to alter in her. She seemed to grow up.

We drove back through the fitful sun. As I pulled

113

up at my house she sat quietly for a minute looking at her hands. 'It's funny,' she said in a low voice. 'When someone hates you in your family you're always tensed – ready for the fight. Then they get sick and everything changes. Suddenly it's finished. You don't have any more enemies.'

CHAPTER 11

It started at Mark David's première in July. It had got hot, hot, hot, and that afternoon the *Standard* was full of headlines about the death of John F. Kennedy Jr and Carolyn Bessette in their biplane off Martha's Vineyard. I read the breathless accounts over sunburned shoulders in the metal, sweaty tube.

Rekindled the Kennedy myth. Amid the glitter of Manhattan's cultural and political elite, no couple shone brighter than John F. Kennedy Jr and his wife Carolyn Bessette. They were the ultimate prize for aspiring hostesses, gossip columnists and paparazzi alike, an irresistible combination of wealth, power and good looks. Like film stars or members of a royal family, their every move was captured, and their secret marriage, three years ago on Cumberland Island, off the coast of Georgia, was a rare triumph over the constant media attention. Only months before they had been captured in a very public spat on the streets of New

York in which Kennedy was seen jerking the engagement ring from his fiancée's finger. But the wedding was portrayed as the most romantic of the year – the 'most eligible bachelor' with his fairytale blonde bride . . .

'They were so golden,' Patty said sombrely. 'I don't see how they could die.'

'Everyone dies.'

'Not them, though.'

She sighed, sitting at the kitchen table, and I was struck by her gravity. Her mother had died three days after we had seen her and it had – quietened her. She had taken the bag of her mother's effects: the cheap, shabby watch with the cracked brown strap, the illegible Boots diary, her thin gold wedding ring, the large black handbag. That day she had been quite silent, but I had heard her weeping in the middle of the night, when I had got up to get some water. It had sounded so wild and unrestrained that I had gone right up to her door with the intention of comforting her – but a catch in her breath, a sense that she was listening to see if she had been heard, stopped me – and I crept back to bed. The next morning she had been red-eyed. But it had remained the one subject that she refused to talk about – and so I didn't either. Looking back, I wonder if I seemed cold to her: to ignore her grief as I did. But she seemed content to deal with it by herself and that made perfect sense to me.

'Well, they were hardly paragons,' I said. I sighed. 'According to the *Mail*, the marriage was on the rocks and he was having an affair.'

Patty pushed her hair wearily back from her face.

'Are you okay?' I said.

She nodded.

'You know you can talk about it,' I said awkwardly. 'It's such a big thing – grief. Not that I know anything about it. But you must be feeling – awful.'

She looked at the table. Her expression was so sad, I thought with surprise. I realised with another pang of surprise that she seemed more attractive that way.

She was already dressed for the première. Her dress, a white cotton halter-neck, clean and sharply ironed, made her look fresh and innocent. That was a new development, too. Since her mother's death she had been dressing differently. She talked less, too – the old stream-of-consciousness had begun to dry up. Her new dignity wrong-footed me. It made me realise that I had always taken my superiority over her for granted.

'I've given up smoking,' she said.

'Have you? That's brilliant. I thought you looked different.'

'Well, it might not work. But I thought I'd try. It's not that hard, actually. I feel more . . .' She thought. 'Glittery.'

'Wow.' What was I feeling? Not jealousy? That was ridiculous. 'Is that a new dress?'

'From Hennes. Do you like it?'

'It's lovely.' She looked, I thought wryly, far better than I would.

Patty pressed her hands on her belly.

'I don't know if I should go.'

'Why not?'

'I'm too stupid.'

'Too stupid for what?'

'For them.'

'For who? Mark David? He invited you!'

'*She* was elegant,' Patty said. She stared at Carolyn Bessette, laughing radiantly through a fan of white hair.

'Didn't make her happy, though, did it?'

'Because I don't belong,' Patty said. She bit tenderly at a scab on her finger. 'I don't know about – books and all that.'

'But that doesn't matter! They don't care about that!'

She met my eyes. 'You only say that because you're part of their world.'

'I don't know if I am, though, really,' I said. 'I never know what to say at parties. Half the time I feel like an idiot. With Mark David, for example. I always think he finds me . . . embarrassing.' I flushed, regretting I had given so much away. But to my surprise Patty's eyes seemed to soften.

'But goodness,' she said. 'You're always so poised!

And he does like you. He was saying the other day how much he admired your writing.'

'Mark *David*?'

'Yes! In the café. When you went to the toilet.'

'Really?' I was absurdly pleased.

Patty nodded. 'And Simone said that you were the kindest person she knew.'

'No,' I said. 'Really?'

'It's funny, isn't it?' Patty said. 'How everyone thinks there's something wrong with them. I know I do. I lie in bed and I want to cry because I'm so bad. Like *bad*, bad! And everyone else seems to be so organised; like they've got a plan. I always think of you like that.'

'God, I'm not,' I said.

In fact, I reflected, opening my wardrobe, none of us had a plan. Mark was crippled by the inhibition he had arrived with at college; he still hugged people sideways on, and he still blushed when Jean-Pierre teased him about women. Jean-Pierre and Simone seemed to be growing further apart as they failed to conceive a baby; and my life was as joyless as ever. When would it get better? How was it that other people could move on and have children and I couldn't? I felt as though I was being punished for a crime I hadn't committed. Which, in a way, I was.

'It's about the dotcom boom,' Patty said, appearing in the doorway. 'His play. I read in the paper.'

'Is it?' I pulled out a dress. 'Sounds good.'

'Will his girlfriend be there?'

'Christine? I'm sure.'

'I don't think she likes me.'

I smiled. 'I wouldn't worry. No one likes *her*.'

'Mark must do.'

'Well, he's an innocent.'

'Is he?'

I stared at her sharply. 'You don't *fancy* him, do you?'

'No!' She looked away, blushing. 'You know, in Kensington Gardens today, I thought: "What have I done with my life?" And I haven't done anything. I haven't done one thing, and I'm thirty-three.'

'You're not.'

'Well, I'm going to be. And there was this little girl with an ice lolly, and I thought: "That's what I want." And I know I won't get it.'

I lowered the dress. 'An ice lolly?'

'No. Children. And a husband.'

'Of course you will. Don't be daft.'

'No.' She shook her head. 'I won't. It's like fate – you can't change it.'

'Now you are being ridiculous,' I said.

The theatre had small velvet chairs and ashtrays banked with gritty grey sand. Boxes climbed like shells to a tiny chandelier. Patty looked around eagerly and studied the programme, turning the pages with care, as if they might crumble.

The Shoe Shine Boy was set in a hotel in Berlin at the end of the pre-war stock market boom. The

120

residents were living the high life. But behind the decadence their marriages were collapsing and their values corroding – cracks exposed by the Crash. It was terrifically clever, a wonderful metaphor for the Internet madness. But it was tender too, and hugely moving, and I clapped wildly as the lights went up. So did Patty: she looked irradiated.

'What did you think?'

'Amazing!'

'It's by far the best he's done.'

I looked back at Patty, struck by her beauty, and realised that the man standing beside us was staring too. She saw him, and bit her lip. It was a more grown-up reaction than I had seen her give before – in the past she would have tossed her head – and for some reason it made me irritable. It was incredible, I thought, how much attention she got. 'Shall we go?' I asked.

She threw me a surprised glance. 'Oh. Yes.' And hurried up.

I had not been to a first-night party before and had no idea what to expect. Certainly not what we found, which was a mass of bodies shrieking at the tops of their voices in a sweaty high-ceilinged room. A makeshift bar was operated at one end by a barman red-faced with heat; grimy windows had been shoved high to reveal a peeling balcony on which people were precariously perched. It smelled, with sweet intimate unpleasantness, of sweat.

As we came to the door the hubbub sank a moment and I saw people were staring at Patty. She blinked. I thought bitterly that I used to be the one who turned heads. 'God,' I said. 'You're getting some attention.'

Someone tapped my arm.

'I thought that was you,' said Jean-Pierre. 'Well?'

'Amazing! Didn't you think?'

'I did. Superb.'

He was smiling, and I stared at him. He reminded me of the time when he had got engaged to Simone: that same profound satisfaction, thankfulness, delight . . .

'What's happened?' I asked.

He grinned wider. It was as if a sun had set behind his face – was beaming through every muscle. 'Simone's pregnant.'

'Oh. My. God.'

He threw up both arms in a victory gesture.

'Oh Jean-Pierre,' I said. Tears had come to my eyes. 'I can't believe it.'

'Come here.' He grabbed me and I breathed in his male scent, smelled his sweat, felt the softness of his cotton shirt, and then I was crying in earnest. 'Where's Simone?' I said.

'Gone to the loo.'

We pulled apart, and I saw Patty. She was by the window tucking her hair behind her ear in an embarrassed gesture. 'Patty,' I called.

She turned, big-eyed. But to my surprise Jean-Pierre's face darkened. He stared at her stonily, and turned back to me. 'Yes,' he said. 'She's coming back any second.'

Patty turned away.

'What . . . ?' I began, but before I could finish Simone came up. She came out of my embrace and pressed my hands to her chest. 'I've never been so happy in my life, never, never, never,' she whispered, and in the wonder of her face I saw her new life unfold. But her eyes were sadder when I met them again.

'This will be you soon,' she said.

'I don't even want kids.'

Her eyes got gentler. 'I want you to.'

I dropped her hands. 'So what did you think of the play?'

'Sad.'

'Sad?'

'Didn't you think so?'

'Simone!' Patty said shyly, and she turned to greet her.

I whispered to Jean-Pierre: 'What's the matter?'

He frowned. 'I don't trust her.'

'Why not?'

'She's trouble.'

'She's *nice*,' I said. 'Why are you being so judge-mental?'

Mark David came out of the crowd. He was carrying a book wrapped in silver paper and looked thin and preoccupied; a moustache of sweat dotted his upper lip. But his face lit up when he saw Jean-Pierre. 'Well?'

'It's superb. Hated the set in the second act.'

'We had problems with that.'

'But loved the music. A classic. Your best yet.'

'I'm honoured. Hello, Lottie.'

'It was brilliant.'

'Thank you.' He smiled, and then his eyes went behind me and stayed there.

'How's your car?' Jean-Pierre asked.

'My car?'

'He pranged it,' Jean-Pierre informed me. 'On the Edgware Road. The absent genius.'

'It's in a garage,' Mark David said. 'I thought you and your friend could join us for supper. If you're free?'

I stared at the non-sequitur. He didn't fancy me, did he? Surely he wouldn't really be interested in me? I went hot. 'Absolutely.'

'Good.' He reared back, like a horse at a fence, and I thought: *perhaps he does*. The warmth grew, as if I had knocked back a tequila.

'I'm so pleased,' Mark said, touching Jean-Pierre's arm, and went across to Simone.

'Do you think he's all right?' I said to Jean-Pierre.

He was also looking at Mark, but with an unreadable expression. The joy in his face was now laced with some form of calculation. 'I don't know,' he said.

Christine, wearing a too-dark foundation and a sundress that emphasised her bony chest, came up. She seemed to have done something to her mouth, maybe injected it with silicone: it looked

124

out of whack. 'I'm dying,' she lamented, fanning herself. 'Did you like the play?'

'Very much,' I said.

'Mm.' Her gaze roamed the room and resettled on me. 'Did I see you in *Tatler*?'

'Oh . . . I think so.'

'Was that your mother with you in the picture?'

'Mm.'

'I *said* to Mark we should go to that party.'

'It was pretty dull.'

'Really? It looked good to me.' She sighed. 'I can't get him *away* from his computer.' She saw Jean-Pierre. 'Oh. *Hi!* How are you? Did you get my messages?'

'Yes. Sorry. I've been snowed under.'

'I hope you can come. It should be great fun.' She grimaced at me. 'The ball I'm organising. I can't tell you what a fag it is.' Her eyes sought Jean-Pierre again. 'But you must come.'

'Thing is, I'm not a great ball-goer. And particularly now, with Simone . . .'

'No excuses! We need men.' She grinned. 'Congratulations.'

'Thanks.'

'You must be thrilled! You never thought you'd have children, did you? Simone must be over the moon.'

'She is.'

'She's quite old now, isn't she? What, forty-two?'

She leaned forward. 'You might hear a little bit

125

of news from us, too, any minute. But I don't want to talk too soon.'

'Oh God,' Jean-Pierre murmured, when she left. 'Tell me they won't get pregnant.'

The party heaved and climbed. I escaped to the balcony. As I watched the velvet dark tremble on the plane trees I felt a longing as untethered as the honks from the street below. Something was missing from my life and I felt on the brink of discovering what it was as I looked out at the strings of white lights, the fragile darkness, the glamour of the night. Then Mark shouted: 'Let's get out of here.'

We broke onto the street as from the hold of a ship. Again I felt the tug of that – emptiness – something missing . . .

'Thank God,' Jean-Pierre said. 'I thought we were stuck with her.'

'Who?'

'Your friend.'

I looked around. Christine was picking fluff from Mark's jacket. Simone was looking at her mobile phone. There was no sign of Patty.

'That's weird!' I exclaimed.

Then the fire door rattled and Patty stepped into a funnel of light. She had put on lipstick: her mouth stood out in the same too-bright red she had worn to see her mother. She seemed nervous. 'Gosh, I'm sorry,' she said. 'I went to the bathroom and I got lost and then the lady sent me the wrong way. Have you all been waiting?'

'Not at all,' Mark said, and Christine tightened her grip on his arm. But Simone smiled and held out her hand. 'Chinese?'

'Oh, yes, please!' Patty cried, and they ran laughing, across the road. We followed more slowly, our differing paces reflecting, I mused, our differing expectations of the meal.

The Friendly Inn had pink and green fairy lights and an off-putting smell of greasy duck. Christine looked as if she expected to catch fleas. But Mark was sitting down quite naturally and Patty was reaching for a menu. 'I love restaurants like this. When I was little my daddy always took me to the Hong Kong Phooey for Sunday lunch,' she said. 'We'd eat crispy duck and have banana fritters, and he'd tell me the hundred rules to live by.'

Mark smiled. 'What were they?'

'Oh, you know: that you always had to make an effort – that was number one. You could never squeal on your mates, but you could screw your enemies – that was number two; and that whisky was the best cure for a broken heart.'

'Is that so,' Jean-Pierre murmured drily.

But Mark looked spellbound. It occurred to me that he was not being polite – he was genuinely interested. He put down his menu. 'He sounds like a character.'

'Oh, he was. Could charm the birds off the trees. He grew up on a ranch in Wyoming. He always gave me a present on Mondays, because he said

127

that was when people needed cheering up; that's when he'd been most miserable on the ranch. He was a children's entertainer. Then he went to jail.'

'Oh. Um. Not for long, I hope?'

'Three years. He was given six. But he got time off for good behaviour. The chaplain said he made the best prison garden he'd seen in twenty years.'

I heard a snort and looked coldly at Jean-Pierre. But it was Christine. She said to Mark. 'Shall we order?'

'Of course.' He put up a hand for the waiter. But when he didn't catch his attention he put it down and turned back to Patty. 'So do you see him?'

'Not really.'

'Ah.'

'It's okay. I'm kind of used to it.'

Christine thrust her arm at the waiter. 'What water do you have?'

'You like still, or sparkling?'

'No, what *kind*? Do you have Perrier?'

'Um. Still or sparkling?'

'No, do you have *Perrier*?'

Prawn crackers and champagne arrived in succession. Mark held up a buzzing glass to Simone. 'To the new arrival! I couldn't be happier for you both.'

Patty looked round. 'The what?'

'Simone's having a baby,' Mark said.

Patty's gaze went from Simone to Jean-Pierre. She seemed almost inordinately surprised. 'Oh, wow.'

'It's the best news,' I said warmly.

Simone smiled joyfully. 'I feel so lucky.' She looked at Jean-Pierre. 'We both do.'

'A baby, though,' said Christine. She plucked up her water. 'Of course, we want one, but I don't know how I'll bear the early starts. Mummy said she didn't get a wink of sleep for ten years after she had me.'

Jean-Pierre raised his eyebrow. Simone laughed. 'I don't care what time it wakes up,' she said. She touched Patty's arm. 'We've been trying for ages. It feels like a miracle.'

Patty grinned at her. Clearly Simone had been added to her pantheon of heroines, up there with Katharine Hepburn and Marilyn Monroe. 'Well, you'll be a terrific mum, no shit. I wish I'd had a mum like you.'

Jean-Pierre raised his eyebrows again. Mark said: 'Would you like children?'

'Oh I'd love them. I'd like six.'

We ate seaweed and duck. Patty told Mark: 'I just read *The Zoo Story*.'

'Did you like it?'

'I loved it.'

'Have you read *Seascape*?'

They fell into a discussion about theatre. Christine turned stiffly to me. 'Is your father still in the south of France?'

'Some of the time. He's in Berlin a lot at the moment.'

'What's he doing there?'

129

'Buying property.'

But her boiled-sweet eyes were fixed on Patty.

'She's nice, isn't she?' I asked mischievously.

'I beg your pardon?'

'Patty. Isn't she nice?'

She looked at her dubiously. 'I suppose so. How did you meet her?'

'In LA. She's an actress.'

'Yes, she said.' She took a sip of wine. 'Mark, is there any more Evian? No, not that one, the other.'

Behind us rose a ragged chorus of whoops and a cheerful rendition of 'Happy Birthday'. A loucheness warmed the air. At the table where they were singing a man stood up, waggled his hips, and began unbuttoning his shirt to slow handclaps.

I couldn't say how it started. All I remember is that Christine was pestering Jean-Pierre about her ball. Mark said something to Patty like, 'You should come along.'

I could see she was pleased and nervous at the same time. She obviously thought he meant it. She bit her lip, glancing at Christine. 'Really?'

'Absolutely,' Mark said heartily. 'Mustn't she, Christine?'

'Hm?'

'Patty must come to the ball.' He was obviously delighted with the idea. 'These charity things can be a bit dull. But it would be wonderful to have you. I'll get you a ticket.'

'Oh. Well,' Christine said. She was quite ruthless about it. 'The thing is, we're full.'

There was a jagged silence. It was clear she was being outrageously snobbish – that there were tickets, but that she had no intention of allowing Patty one. She turned to Simone. 'But what are your plans for childcare? My friend runs a really good agency, if you want the number. They're in Knightsbridge.'

'But there is room,' Mark said.

Behind him the raucous table burst into a drunken cheer. Christine straightened her fork. She looked directly at Patty. 'No, we're sold out,' she said. 'After all, it's just for friends.'

She couldn't have spelled it out more clearly. Patty was not one of them; she didn't make the grade. Her neck came up in red blotches. She raised a jerky glass of champagne and spilled a drop on her chin. I felt absolutely mortified. A blush came up on my cheeks.

Jean-Pierre had picked up his own champagne. 'Balls,' he said, flicking a hand. He looked at Mark. 'Was that play two hours?'

'One and a half,' Mark said. He looked back at Christine. 'But there is room.'

'Really, it's fine,' Patty protested.

He shook his head. 'There is room. Isn't there?'

'No,' Christine said.

Their eyes met and held.

There was another pause. 'Actually,' Simone said, 'I don't think I'm going to be able to make your ball either.'

Christine looked shocked. 'But –'

'I'm sorry,' Simone said. She looked gravely at Christine, and then at Jean-Pierre. She loathed snobbishness; she didn't need to say more. 'I think we need to go. I'm feeling a bit ill.'

'I'm sorry,' Jean-Pierre said to Mark in a low voice. 'The play was superb. Let me know what I owe you.'

'It's wonderful about the baby.'

'Thanks. I'll call tomorrow.'

With an awkward goodbye they moved to the door.

'I'm going to the toilet,' Patty said.

'Are you okay?' I asked. But she was threading her way through the tables, her head down. Her purse lay on the table, its cheap black nylon seeming to symbolise her humiliation.

As soon as she was out of earshot Mark turned a burning gaze on Christine. 'How dare you?'

Christine stared. 'Me? How dare *you* flirt with that cheap tart?'

'I wasn't!' His hands were shaking with anger; he clasped them.

'You were!' Suddenly her eyes were wet with tears. 'Mark?' she asked fearfully. But he shook her hand off.

The waiter arrived. 'Any puddings?' he asked. 'Coffee?'

'Just the bill.'

We sat in silence while he went to get it. Finally Patty came back to the table. She had wiped off her lipstick and pinned up her hair. Her face had

132

a blurred, smeared look. But she seemed to be in control. 'That was the best duck I've ever had,' she said. 'And this restaurant, I think it must be really like a restaurant in China. The waiter said they had fortune cookies, but I' – her voice faltered and sang – 'I said next time.'

'Come and sit down,' Mark said gently. He pulled out her chair. 'Simone and Jean had to go. I'm just getting the bill.'

'Oh,' Patty said. She sat herself like a child and brought the edges of her cardigan together protectively. 'I think those fritters were the end of me. My mum always said I didn't know when to stop.'

The sob seemed to take her by surprise. It rose sharply in her throat – and then she was weeping wildly. I remember thinking in some vague way that it was probably good for her to get it out – that it was because of her mother. But Mark looked horrified. He looked as if he would happily sink through the floor. 'I'm so sorry,' he kept saying. 'Forgive me. I'm so sorry.'

At last we were in the street. 'What a night!' I said in an attempt at humour. 'I'm sorry it was so – But congratulations, Mark. I really thought the play was brilliant.'

'No, I feel responsible.' He hardly heard me. He was looking at Patty: his glasses caught the street-light. 'May I see you home?'

'Honestly,' I said. 'We'll be fine. We'll grab a cab.'

'No, please. Let me. Here –' He threw out his

hand for a cab, but it was taken. He stepped into the road, searching hopelessly for another.

Then the tramp loomed up. His grey hair stuck out like feathers; his nose was pitted with drink. A wen clung under his eye, which fixed in awe on Patty. 'Pretty,' he breathed, raising a wavering hand. He sounded like he had an inch of water on his lungs.

Patty cringed. 'Go away!'

He leaned closer, with an inarticulate murmur of admiration.

'No!' she shrieked. 'Get him *away*!'

Then she was running blindly at the traffic.

A car screeched to a halt: I glimpsed a terrified woman's face at the wheel. 'Sorry!' I cried to Mark and Christine, and went after her. She ran clumsily, her bag banging against her hip, down one road, then another; I caught up with her outside a sex shop, in an alley. She was sobbing against a wall. 'Everything's ruined!'

'He's just a tramp!'

It had begun to rain and I waited with a mixture of pity and irritation until she wiped her nose on her hand and then blew it on a dirty bit of tissue.

'I'm okay now.'

'Sure?'

'Yes. But I'm going to – walk.'

She was so determined that I left her. I got a cab on Regent Street and rattled home past the crowds at the bus stops, the romantic couples, the drunken groups of youths. But when I got to the house I saw with disbelief that the night was not yet at an end. A silhouette shadowed the path and I thought for a wild second it was Jean-Pierre. He was as thickly built, but when I came up I saw that his tan was deep as a game show presenter's on that heavy summer night.

'Ma'am, we've met before,' he said. 'I didn't mean to scare you.'

It was Ed Kaplan.

CHAPTER 12

Charm is a shield. Like nettles, which grow only where the earth has been dug, it exists alongside danger and disturbance. Kaplan had charm in spades that night and it frightened me. I had seen Patty's broken thumb and the way she had quivered in her yellow duster coat.

I said: 'She's not here, I'm afraid.'

'Where is she?' As if he saw he had been too abrupt, he raised his hands pacifically. 'I'd sure like to see her. I do apologise. I know I'm late. I hope I didn't scare you.'

I thought of the call-girl he had been linked to – the way he had ordered Patty into the lift. I felt a thrum of fear. 'Well, the thing is,' I said, 'she's not actually here.'

Kaplan blinked and twitched his lips, as if the statement was something he had been dreading. Then he licked his lips. 'I wonder if I might come in and rest, then, a minute? If I might ask that favour?'

He took his hand out of his pocket and I saw it, too, was bandaged. As he rubbed his forehead I realised he looked exhausted. His cheeks sagged, outlined cartoonishly in shadow, and his eyes seemed to droop. 'I've been flying all night,' he said. He turned his head, a ray of humour lightening his blue eyes. 'I've had a challenging week.'

'It's probably best not,' I said.

'See,' he said in a soft voice, which fell, softly, like a lullaby, 'I could really use your bathroom.'

I hesitated. I was clear that Patty shouldn't see him; but what might she say if she heard I had turned him away?

He gave a crooked smile. 'If I promise not to eat you?'

'Well, just quickly,' I said, and got out my keys.

When he came back from the loo he seemed to have done something to himself – regained his charisma, his bursting masculinity. But in the bright light he still looked a decade older. 'What am I doing?' he said. 'I haven't introduced myself. I'm Ed Kaplan.'

He put out his hand, not the bandaged one, and I saw a white strip where a wedding ring had been. He smelled of soap and bar smells – cigarette smoke, cigars. His grip was strong and cold.

'Yes,' I said. 'We met before. Would you like some water?'

'That would be a kindness.'

He sat and watched me pour it.

'Nice place.'

'Thank you.'

'Been here long?'

'Three years.'

He made little sucking sounds as he drank. 'I was reading on the plane about some movie they're making round here.'

'*Notting Hill.*'

'Should raise the property prices.'

'I should think so.'

His eyes fell on a pile of letters on the table. 'DEPARTMENT OF COLPOSCOPY,' the top one read. 'Dear Miss Bell, Your doctor has referred you to the above outpatient clinic. Your consultant has reviewed the referral . . .'

He tore his gaze away. 'This is a great part of town,' he said with an effort. 'I've only stayed downtown before.'

'Oh, really? In – the centre?'

He didn't seem to hear: his stare had taken on a keener quality. 'You were at the Beverly Hills,' he said. 'Last summer.'

I felt another twinge of fear. 'That's right.'

But he just nodded. 'Thought I knew the face.' His eyes were still scrutinising me. 'You an old friend?'

'No, that was when we met.'

'That so?' He slotted a fingernail between his teeth: took it out when his phone started ringing. 'Excuse me. I'll have to take this. Yes? No . . . No sir. Well, you can tell her that's just jack shit.'

He hung up. His eyes locked on me and in their pale blue I felt a strange stir, a churning in my stomach. 'I'll be straight with you,' he said. 'I'm here for Patty. You know how she's feeling?'

He meant about him. I shook my head. 'I'm afraid not.'

'She going to be long?'

'She might not even be back.'

He let out a breath. In his fingers the glass hung like a thimble. He said: 'She got a new boyfriend?'

'You'd have to ask her.'

'We had a little bust-up last time we met. She mention that?'

'No.'

'That so?' His eyes tested this information. 'See, I'm in sort of a fix. And I need to speak to Patty.' He licked his lips again. 'There's something about that girl,' he said in a different voice. 'You can't get her out of your head.'

'It's true,' I agreed weakly. It had occurred to me that Patty might be upset I had let him in. It was odd that she hadn't mentioned their fight. I understood for the first time that there might be gaps in her artless accounts.

As if overcome by tiredness, Kaplan's elbow slipped from the table. 'My wife left me,' he said. 'Took my girls.' He drew his hand raspingly over his chin. 'It's been quite a month.'

I felt frightened. I suddenly knew, with absolute clarity, that Patty would not want him in the house. I thought of the way he had been that day at the pool – the scandal with the call-girl. Patty's broken thumb – I got to my feet. 'If you don't mind, I think you'd better go now.'

'Right now?'

'If you don't mind.'

'Sure,' he said. But he didn't move. 'You must have been in love once upon a time?' he asked. 'Pretty girl like you?'

'I really think you should go.'

I was hot with shame. One o' clock in the morning – wherever she had gone she would surely be back soon. What had I been thinking of? And she was in such a state . . . 'I'll tell her you came,' I promised wildly.

But he just crossed his legs. 'See, I've come a long way.'

'You can leave her a message. I can give her your number.'

A key scraped in the door.

Kaplan put down his glass and came to his feet. He put his hands in his pockets, and then took them out again.

'He's quite, I suppose,' we heard Patty's voice agree cheerfully.

The front door slammed. 'Well, he's got a great arse,' said another voice. Tyrone.

They burst in and Patty's face shut like a door. She threw me one amazed look of betrayal.

'Ooh, fab,' exclaimed Tyrone. He danced in, wearing a tight sleeveless T-shirt emblazoned "dirtywhiteboy". 'I was freezing my tits off out there. Oh, Jesus. Not you.'

Kaplan was staring at Patty.

She turned frantically. 'Why's he here?'

I bit my lip. 'I'm sorry – he was at the door –'

'Go *away*!' Her hands felt blindly at her neck. 'Make him *go away*!'

Tyrone was shaking his head in disgust. 'You've got a fucking cheek!'

'Now, now Patsy,' Kaplan soothed. He took a slow step towards her, putting up his hand to Tyrone – not the bandaged one, the other. 'I just want to talk. I don't want no fight.'

'You already had a fight! You already gave me a fight! I told you I don't want to see you! I told you that!'

'But that was just because you were mad, baby doll. You didn't mean it.'

'I did!' She turned wildly, her hip slamming on the counter. 'He *hit* me!'

'Well, that's not right true, honey. You were hitting *me*.' He raised both hands, as if to prove his honourable intentions.

'Tosser,' hissed Tyrone.

'See, you have to see it from my point of view,' Kaplan observed. 'It was hard for me. When the FBI got on my back. And you left that message for Betsey. She just went sheer crazy. I ain't seen my little girls for weeks. She's just mad with misery.'

Patty's neck was blotched – with hurt or anger, I couldn't be sure. She clutched her hair. 'I believed you *again* and you did it *again*!'

'Well, but honey,' Kaplan said. 'You weren't right calm, now, were you. And then you know, that message. Betsey was on the floor. She had to go to hospital. But I've come to give you everything you want. The house, the clock, the kids. You can have them all.'

Patty was white as if he had a gun to her head. 'That's what you said before! It's another lie, another lie!'

'And I trusted you, so I guess neither of us did real well. But when you left I hunted for you all over! I went to Minnie's, and Jack's, even that goddamn psychic!'

I felt sick of the whole thing suddenly. 'I'm going to bed.'

Patty snapped at my arm. 'You said you *loved* me!' she sobbed to Kaplan, and now it was the wail of an abandoned child. 'You said you'd love me forever!'

'And I will! When I get the FBI off my tail!'

As if this was somehow the final straw, Patty screamed: 'Tell him to go!'

We stared.

She smashed a plate to the floor. 'Tell him to *go*!'

For a moment we were frozen – then Kaplan fell to his knees. His faced seemed tremendously wrecked, as if someone had taken a myriad of small pickaxes to his face. 'Don't do this,' he begged. 'My wife has left me. My career's shot. The house is gone. I'm facing ruin. Do you understand? I'm facing ruin!'

'I don't give a fuck,' Patty cried. 'Just go! Go! Go! Go!'

I couldn't look at him. Because it was evident

that whatever he had done, whatever she had done, he had loved her. She was his last hope, or perhaps his first hope, and whatever she had done to him was as bad as whatever he had done to her. But I said, because I had no choice: 'I think you'd better go.'

'Yes,' Tyrone confirmed gleefully. He cocked his thumb. 'Beat it, ducky!'

With a terrible look of defeat, Kaplan got to his feet. 'Then understand this,' he told her back. 'You cannot talk. I'll go, but you cannot talk. I'll leave my cell,' he added in a low voice to me – but Patty heard.

'Get *out*!' she screamed, and it was without more words that I saw him to the door. It had begun to rain: the air smelled of earth. He knocked his bandaged hand clumsily against the door with a sharp intake of breath. Then he was walking up the street and into the night.

The next morning we heard that Simone had miscarried.

CHAPTER 13

The copywriter and I got back together in July and we went on holiday to Sicily. I came back at the end of the month and found his message on the answer-phone. He was asking if she might like to see the new Mamet.

The story soon came out.

'See, he called the day after you left about one of your interviews,' Patty said, 'and we ended up talking about his play. Because it was so good and everything. And he said did I want to go to F- F- that bookshop on the Charing Cross Road.'

'Foyles.'

'Yes. And I said okay, because I didn't have any plans that night.' She flicked me a glance. 'And a guy tried to feel me up, outside, and Mark looked after me. And he was really sweet, and said did it happen a lot, and I said, well, sometimes, and he said he wasn't surprised, because I was so beautiful.' Her face lit with remembered joy and she ducked her head. 'And I said well, I didn't *feel* beautiful, and he said was I happy, and I said no, and he said nor was he, and we ended up going for a curry and talking all night.' She peered at me. 'You're cross.'

I stood and began putting dishes in the dishwasher – Patty's dirty dishes. Or perhaps both of theirs – I noticed two eggcups paired neatly by the sink. 'I see,' I said.

A rabbity expression had come over Patty's face. She ran her finger over her thumb. 'You are, aren't you?'

'No. But did you not do the dishes?'

'Oh, well, I meant to, you see, but, um, I got back later than I thought.'

'You did pay the cleaner.'

'Oh, yes, I remembered that. She wants more Flash.'

In silence I continued to stack the dishwasher. She watched me, twisting her hands.

'I didn't mean it to happen,' she said in a small voice. 'I thought you'd be *pleased* for me.'

'It's amazing how things just happen with you, isn't it?'

'You *said* I should find someone nice!'

'But not someone else's boyfriend! Jesus, Patty, how much *more* wreckage are you going to cause?'

Tears sprang to her eyes. 'I'm not! I don't!'

'Well, you seem to.'

She stared at me, betrayed. 'That's not fair! I haven't done anything! He never loved Christine! He's left her!'

'Well, I assumed he had done that at least.'

Silence. She looked at the floor. Eventually I said, 'Has he been staying here?'

145

'No.' She bit her thumb. 'Only once.' She peered over at me. 'I honestly didn't mean it to happen.'

'That's not the point.'

'You *wanted* him to leave Christine.'

'I didn't want you to bloody break them up!' I turned to face her. 'I mean, what on earth do you have in common?'

She frowned. Drew herself up. 'Quite a lot. Actually.'

The phone went and she raised her hand.

'*I'll* get it,' I snapped.

But it was him.

The next morning I drove down to my mother's in Gloucestershire. I came back to find Patty coming down the stairs dragging a full bin liner. She froze when she saw me. 'Oh, hi.'

The hall was stuffy and hot. A fly buzzed weakly on the floor. I wondered suddenly if she was moving out.

'Hi there,' I said. I put down my bag.

'Oh, hi,' she said again. She bit her lip.

'Are you . . . off out?'

'Um, yes. Just . . . going out.'

The fly launched itself into the air. It dropped on its back and whirred faintly.

'So how are you?'

'Um. Good, thanks.'

She looked radiant. In the dusky light her skin glowed. Her brow was clear. As I watched a shaft of sunlight found her face and lit the fine hairs on its surface.

'You look well.'

'Thank you.'

'Do you want some tea?'

She blinked. 'Okay.'

We went into the kitchen. It felt chill and dead – unused since I was away. I opened the French doors and an avalanche of sun crashed in.

Patty hovered by the door.

'It's all right!' I exclaimed. 'I'm not going to eat you.'

'Really?'

I threw her look. 'Come on,' I said. 'Let's hear the gory details.'

She gave a grateful smile. 'Oh, Lottie, I'm so happy. I think I've finally found him. The person I've been searching for all my life.'

I looked at her. 'Mark *David*?'

'He's *so amazing*.' She came over to me pleadingly. 'You know he got a first at Oxford.'

'I did, funnily enough.'

'And he's won *prizes*. And his books are *so amazing*. And he's read everything in the world, practically. And he doesn't care about my past. And he says I have to keep away from Ed Kaplan. And he's really gentle. The other day, at the station, I wanted to buy a magazine. And he said, fine, and he just sat down and waited for me.'

'Well, what else would he do?'

'I don't know – like, Ramzi would have been really angry and said we didn't have time. And

147

Mark won't let me pay for anything. And he keeps telling me I'm beautiful.'

'Well, you are.'

'And he never criticises me. I can't believe it!' Her face was stunned with gratitude – she couldn't believe her luck. It was transubstantiation, I thought. *And this bread signifies the heavenly food and divine perfections. So he that eateth of this bread acquires heavenly bounty, and the divine light, and partakes of Christ's perfections, and thereby gains everlasting life.* It made me think that I was incapable of that kind of gratitude to a man. That wholehearted thankfulness. Or love. Why was that? 'And he says I'm sexy twenty times a day!' she was saying. 'And he protects me! I can't believe how different he is from Ramzi. Or –' She left the thought unfinished. 'And he thinks I'm really talented.'

'And you fancy him?'

Her eyes slid away. 'Yes.'

'Really?'

She rubbed her nose. 'I mean, it's not like a hurricane, you know, like some big crashing wave, like I had with Ed. But it's – calm. Nice.'

'Nice.'

'Well, yes, and he really worries about pleasing me. He's like, "Is it all right?" It's sweet. And he is – sort of sexy. Without his glasses he's like a peeled onion, all white and pale and tired-looking; he gets this sore bit on his nose and his eyes are all small, and pleading; and he wears these blue silk pyjamas and he has really soft skin, like a –'

I put up a hand. 'Enough.'

She giggled. 'I keep thinking he'll get angry. But he never does. He seems to actually like being with me. He never gets cross when I talk. He says, "I like hearing you." Last night I cooked him fish.'

'*You* did?'

'Well – he did. I made the salad. And we watched *Some Like It Hot*. He knows everything about Marilyn Monroe. He wrote a long story about her. She had this disease that meant she couldn't have children.'

'Endometriosis.'

'And she was in pain the whole time. Can you believe it? It must have been awful.'

'And what about Ed?'

'What about him?' Her face was blank.

I sighed. 'And what about Christine?'

'Oh, she's being really mean. She told Simone I was a tramp. She wants him to give her the house.'

'The one in Chelsea?'

'Mm. He says he's going to. He says he just wants a quiet life. He says his life feels like it's finally making sense.' She frowned suddenly, as at an uncomfortable thought. 'Anyway,' she said, 'I'm so happy you're not cross. I was really frightened.'

'Oh, well. If it makes you both happy.'

She smiled and in that moment all life seemed to turn inside her – her face was the quintessence of loveliness, a synaesthetic study in beauty

149

– eyes, hair, mouth forming a perfect whole. I sometimes think of her then – as she was at that minute, like the Nasdaq, at the height, before it began its fall. She drowned me in a hug. 'I love you,' she said.

'And I love you too,' I said.

And I did.

Had I been doing a case study on the effect of a certain type of relationship on a certain type of girl, I could not have found a better subject than Patty. In those first days of her relationship with Mark David she adopted a bizarre new wardrobe: high-necked blouses that made her breasts big as balloons, stuffy skirts that hung below the knee, loafers. She even walked more primly and put up her hair.

Her habits changed with her wardrobe. The self-help books were bundled into her wardrobe in a pink Miss Selfridge bag and she began poring over the American classics instead – *Lolita*, *The Grapes of Wrath*, *Portrait of a Lady*. I was intrigued to see that she actually finished them – she went through them laboriously, intently, pausing to consult her new dictionary *(To an exquisite lexicographer, with all love.)* The books seemed to make her even more serious, and I would catch a look of abstracted intentness on her face when I walked in on her unawares. She particularly liked *Portrait of a Lady*, which she read twice, and then she began on the poetry. She surprised me there. She seemed to find genuine pleasure in my Yeats and Auden, and then I began to find books around the house that even I had never heard of – by Sharon Olds, Dunbar, Rilke.

Mark David's picture was propped above her bed. He stared seriously in tortoiseshell glasses from the cheap black frame, looking thinner and younger and more optimistic, the way he did when I first knew him. Beside it lay a dried rose.

'He gave it to me that first night. Wasn't that sweet? He's always giving me things. And you'll never guess what he said the other night. That he doesn't think he's good enough for *me*.' She stared, wide-eyed. 'Were you this happy with your husband?'

'I don't know.'

'I suppose it's hard to remember. Do you still see him?'

'No.' I replied.

'Oh.' She touched my arm comfortingly. 'I keep dreaming about my wedding day. Amongst all the flowers, in the country.' She paused. 'You know Mark wouldn't sleep with me for days?'

'Charming.'

'Oh, no, but it was. Because he said he didn't think I was ready. He said, "I want you to feel relaxed." And when I told him I didn't usually come, because I got so nervous, and I kind of felt like I was just a body for men, sometimes, he stared at me really seriously, and said, "We must make sure that never happens again." And then when I did come he looked me in the eyes and I thought: "No man has ever done that to me before." Do you know what I mean?'

'I don't know.' It occurred to me that no man had ever spoken remotely like that to me – and that I had never looked a man in the eye during sex. A parallel emotional universe veered in front of me, like a bank of cloud at a plane window, grew thinner, and disappeared.

'And you know what else he said?'

'Amaze me.'

'"Let me in." I said, "What do you mean?" He said, "You're not letting me in." And, you know, I wasn't. Because I felt so, like, I don't know, like he would be another cunt, or something. Last night he said to me, "You epitomise femininity."' She smiled dreamily. 'Do you know what "epitomise" means?'

'I should really get on with my book. It's two o' –'

'D' you think he'll go off me?'

'Off you? Why would he?'

'I don't know.' She sighed. 'Men always seem to. They start really keen and say they'll love me forever and never leave and then they always do and I never know why.'

'Well, he's pretty steady.'

'That's true.'

And she clasped her hands with a kind of wistful hope.

That August *The Shoe Shine Boy* was transferred

to Broadway and Mark David went to New York. This partition introduced an exhilarating yearning to the romance. Patty mooned over his letters, smoothing the pages as she had smoothed the programme for his play. She laboured over her replies, checking her dictionary, or me, for spellings and consulting earnestly on grammar. Going into her bedroom for eyelash curlers one day I found one of his letters on the bed. I couldn't resist. The page crackled as I picked it up by the corner – he had used old-fashioned blue airmail paper.

Dearest Patsy,
  My darling girl,
  New York reeks, and as I walk the tunnelled streets – they want me to use a limo, but I refuse; air seems impossible to come by in this city – my body aches for you and the missing of you strains my limbs until they crack. I look up and the strip of sky, far above, smashing hard blue, beats like a far-off freedom, the freedom I will feel when you are back next to my heart. My dear, I never thought we would [this word I could not decipher] together as we have. It feels as if I have been plucked from the ledge where I was crouched in a funk, tensed to spring, and placed in a milky bath attended by goddesses – one goddess – you. Dearest, the idea of finding another woman attractive is so far from my heart. American producers are

Hitlers in drag. Esme is the worst kind,
hectoring and desperate at the same time; I
swear I keep away from her. Have you finished
Breakfast At Tiffany's? Did you get the part?
I long to see you in one of my plays. I have
begun to write the piece we talked about. It
will be the best thing I have done; it is flowing
from me like a river. You are my inspiration –
my Galatea. I love you – I love you – I love
you.

I have to go out again now, to drink a gin
and tonic with a Palestinian writer who claims
to be a fan. If he only knew my limitations
and my accursed weakness – I will try to tell
him and he will not listen . . .

Christine has gone silent.

With all my heart I love you. You have trans-
formed my life in a way I had given up all
hope of
MMD.

I left without the curlers; the shock persisted all
week. I think it was at the extent of his infatu-
ation. But also at the force of his love: it had been
so long since I had felt it myself I had forgotten
how it could be. That night I had a fight with the
copywriter and came home alone.

Those late summer days I hardly saw her. As
the leaves began to fall and the shadows length-
ened I felt like we were figures in a weather
house, her out and smiling, me in and closeted

away – a face for her to greet as she clattered down the stairs, off to some dinner or picnic, often with Jean-Pierre and Simone, when Mark David flew back for the weekend. My conversations with her dwindled, edged, like mourning paper, with unspoken resentments. I never went out and seemed to have no friends; the phone rang endlessly for her. As the copywriter and I had broken up again, I spent the nights writing my novel in my study listening to distant shouts of laughter from the pub.

'That girl seems to be stealing your life,' my mother observed sharply on the phone.

I gave a dismal laugh. 'I know.'

'I keep telling you, you've got to stop being a doormat.'

I even began to read Patty's self-help books.

In September Patty went to stay with Mark in New York; a couple of weeks later *Harper's* asked me to go there to interview Twiggy. I didn't want to call Patty. But I was lonely. *Plus ça change*, I thought bitterly, recalling that LA afternoon we had met.

'Oh, *hi*,' she said warmly down the phone, and I felt relieved that she was pleased to hear from me. 'It's great here! It's like a big buzzing factory; I just love it so much! And the waiters are so sweet, and the rowboats in Central Park are so cute, and I even want to get up in the morning – you know how I used never to be able to get up. You should see us. We have such a sweet flat. We're like an old married couple. Guess what we bought today? Cushions! What? You're *in* New York? Why didn't you *say?*'

I took a cab uptown along the humid, caramel-sweet avenues. The apartment was in a blank-faced block by the park. I don't recall if I was early. But there was an extended wait when I rang the bell.

Finally Mark David's voice buzzed tinnily through the brass grille. 'Lottie! Fourth floor.'

I found him in a towelling dressing gown with shaving foam on his his jaw. 'We're running late,' he said, laughing, as he bent to kiss me, and it was the laugh that really struck me – I had never seen him laugh unselfconsciously before. Then Patty appeared behind him. She was in bare feet and a red dress. It was silk, knotted at the shoulder – fluid, expensive. 'Lottie!'

Mark stared at her. 'You look like a film star!'

'Do you like it?' She smiled shyly at me. 'It's new,' she said.

He reached for her mouth. 'It's sublime.'

I looked politely away. Aside from a pair of red fake fur cushions – the new purchases, presumably – the apartment was dull and corporate-neutral. Slatted blinds fidgeted at the windows. Gold-framed photographs of pebbles decorated the walls. A large TV crouched in a corner, and one entire wall was a smoked-glass mirror. On the pine coffee table I made out an asparagus steamer sailing in a boat of white tissue. A pile of hardbacks climbed beside it: *Birthday Letters* by Ted Hughes, *Collected*

Fictions by Jorge Luis Borges, a paperback called *Blinded By The Right*; also *Mars and Venus In The Bedroom*.

Patty followed my gaze. 'We buy a book a day. It's our new thing.' She smiled over at Mark. 'And we have a cocktail every evening at six pm.'

'Which is why I'm putting on so much weight,' Mark said. He belted his dressing gown. 'I must make myself presentable. Lottie will think we never get up.'

'Well, we don't,' Patty said.

He bent again to kiss her. He still hadn't mastered the full-on kiss, I saw: it was more of a peck. Then his long white legs vanished into the bedroom and Patty sank onto a sofa. She pulled up a foot to pick at her yellow heel. 'I can't believe you're here! How is everything? How's Buster?' (She meant the ginger cat.) 'Is the house all right? Did my cornflowers grow in the garden? Because I heard London was really rainy. It's been so hot here you wouldn't believe it; it feels like another world; I can hardly remember England.'

'Well, you've not been missing much. The weather's been absolutely foul.'

'How's the boy?'

'Oh. We broke up.'

'Oh no! What, for good?'

'Oh, I don't know. Maybe. Hopefully. He's just not worth it.'

'But he seems really nice!'

I gave her a look.

'Anyway,' I said. 'So. This is your flat.'

She smiled. 'Isn't it cute? I just feel so happy here. Every morning I wake up and it's like I've got a, I don't know, a band of gold around my heart; I can't explain; I just feel so happy. I've never felt like that before. And Mark's so affectionate. And he's just so . . . nice. And he's been taking me to galleries. Yesterday we went to the Whitney and saw this amazing exhibition on art and culture during the century; what was it called? Anyway. But it's just so nice to be back in America. I like the energy. I walked along the street yesterday and this black woman stopped and went: "You go, girl!"'

'What did she mean by that?'

'I don't know! I think she liked my dress. But Mark knows such amazing people. We've been going out every night.' She smiled reminiscently. 'Are you doing an interview?'

'Yes, with Twiggy – the model.'

'Oh, she's doing a show, isn't she? We met her the other night. And you know Mark's buying a loft in SoHo?' She sighed. 'I'm so happy.'

'So I see.'

She winked. 'He's learning on the other front, too.'

'Patty!'

'Oh, he can't hear. But Christine's being a bitch. She says the house isn't enough.'

'Why on earth not?'

'Says she's given him her best years. "Her

bitterest years," he says. You know she wouldn't let him sleep with her for a whole year after his fling?'

'His fling?'

'He had a one-night stand. Just a silly little thing. Last year. She went on and on about it. Said he'd broken her trust. She made the house into a prison, he says. No love or affection. He says it was like being on – where was Nelson Mandela?'

'Robben Island.'

'Exactly. And he's so generous. He keeps buying me clothes.' She glanced at her dress. But then a frown came over her face, as if at an unpleasant thought, and she smoothed the fabric with her ugly hand. 'So it's hard,' she murmured.

'Why?'

Mark swung jauntily out of the bedroom. 'Who's for a drink?' he demanded. 'Lottie, you'll have one of the house Rossinis?'

'Sure,' I said. I stared. He was in new, stylish clothes – a blue cashmere jersey and cream trousers. His movements were confident. He seemed far more attractive. 'What's a Rossini?'

'Strawberry and champagne. It's remarkably good.'

Patty turned on the sofa. 'And strawberry liqueur.'

'Except we couldn't find any.'

'No, but I got some kirsch.'

'Which we are *not* going to use.'

He squeezed into the galley kitchen and began to chop strawberries. Patty came out chewing one, dripping pink juice down her fingers. 'Oh, I booked Chez Es Saada.'

He put down his knife. 'You are officially the cleverest girl in the world.'

'And *you* are the cleverest boy.'

Never had I felt quite so alone.

The next day was baking hot. In the hairdryer air the concrete from the pavement seemed to rise and mesh, invisibly, with the tarmac fumes, the caramel peanuts, the dirt and exhaust. In Central Park the grass was yellow as straw in the unremitting noon and downtown, in SoHo, the shop fronts seemed to double as radiators, flashing heat at the steely sky. The entire capitalist edifice seemed to have become a frying pan in which its inhabitants sizzled and snapped, and only the faint shadow at the back of the loft made life seem bearable. Mark threw open the living room windows to let in a weak breath of air and his steps echoed as he picked his way across the sawdust floor, dotted with sanding machines, ice cream wrappers and planks of wood.

'Very much a work in progress,' he said.

'But the floor looks a lot better,' said Patty.

'So when did you buy it?'

'Two months ago.' Mark looked at Patty. 'We fell in love with it.'

'It was the first place we saw.'

With a hiss the lift announced its arrival, and the steel doors opened. Jean-Pierre stood framed in the diminutive box. He stepped from it and shoved his hands in his pockets. 'Hello,' he said.

Patty tucked her hair behind her ear; Mark strode forward. 'Hello! Come in! Did you find it all right?'

'Yes, thanks,' Jean-Pierre said. Sweat darkened his cotton shirt under the arms; he had cut his hair, and his face looked thin. 'So this is it?' he said flatly.

'This is it!' Mark looked round, as if seeing the place anew through his eyes. 'Still a work in progress.'

'Hello,' I said, and Jean-Pierre's damp cheek touched mine. 'So you're doing an interview?' he asked.

'And Patty,' Mark urged, ushering her forward. He watched like a proud parent as they kissed each other hello.

Jean-Pierre stepped away with ill-concealed dislike. 'It's a great place. So are you moving in?'

'Well, that's not certain.' Mark put his arm around Patty and looked at her. 'We haven't made up our minds. But I'd certainly like to. And I think you –'

'Oh, I'd like to,' said Patty, and looked at Jean-Pierre. She walked towards the window.

'The views,' Mark exclaimed, 'are spectacular. Come. See – right across the Hudson.'

I followed them to the line of windows. In the sickly breeze New York simmered like a brick blanket, stretching to the fingers-width of river, an indistinct brown in the distance.

'My hotel's just there,' Jean-Pierre said, and Patty's eyes lifted to him with the same jarring flare of hostility. Below us the heads inched up the concrete, next to the flashing, beetling line of cars. Faint honks popped into the air, and as I watched a bicycle, minute as a fly, bisected the cars and folded on its side. A little crowd converged like filings; then its rider detached itself and several filings congealed and carried him from our eye-line.

'That's bad,' Mark said.

'He should look more carefully,' Jean-Pierre said.

'It might not have been his fault,' Patty said. She turned to Jean-Pierre with cool eyes. 'It might have been a mistake.'

'Then he should have known better,' Jean-Pierre said curtly.

His tone was equally hard, and Mark stared in surprise. Then, as if he had grasped something, he laid a gentle hand on his arm. 'Sometimes people don't know better,' he said softly. 'Accidents happen. We have to have faith.'

Jean-Pierre gave a tiny irritated movement. 'So show me round,' he said. 'This is going to be the kitchen?'

'The kitchen,' Mark agreed. He threw a glance at Patty, clear as if he'd spoken aloud: *he's upset – still not over the baby* – and strode after him. 'And this is the spare bedroom,' his voice went on, diminishing. Their footsteps faded.

I turned to Patty. 'Are you okay?'

She had her forehead on the cool glass; now she turned away with an uncharacteristic exasperation, fanning her flushed face with her hand. 'Never mind!' she burst out.

'Patty?'

She came to a stop in the middle of the room and I saw that she was crying. 'He hates me,' she whispered.

'Of course he doesn't hate you!'

It was on the tip of my tongue to say that he didn't know her – or care either way. But before I could even voice this to myself she had shaken her head. 'He does! He thinks I'm trash!'

'Of course he doesn't!'

'He does! And it's all because of –'

The rising sound of the men's voices made her break off.

'Because of what?' I demanded.

But she just shook her head as if she wished she hadn't said anything. 'Maybe we should go,' she said. She went across to Mark and clutched his arm. 'Maybe we should go,' she repeated.

'Too hot, darling?' Mark asked. He touched her cheek. 'Well – let's have lunch.'

As we vied to make our excuses he looked at us with mild hurt. 'But of course,' he told himself, 'you're both busy. Lottie, it was lovely to see you. Jean, we'll meet tomorrow.'

'Certainly.' He smiled miserably at Mark David. 'But I'm a pig. I haven't asked about the play.'

'It's wonderful.'

'I can't wait to see it on Broadway. It's where it belongs.'

'I think so.'

'The staging okay?'

'Very good.'

'And are you working on anything new?'

'A piece about Patty.' Mark put a proud hand on her waist.

'I see.'

'The flat is lovely,' I said.

In the lift we stood so close I could smell the heat of his skin and see the the way the blond hairs curled messily on his neck above his fraying collar. 'So how are you?' I said quietly.

He shrugged and I saw his nails were bitten to the quick. 'Not too bad. Never been a great fan of New York.'

'How's Simone?'

'Bearing up. Sorry. I mean: she's cut up.' Realising that he was too abrupt, he turned to face me. 'She's taking it hard.'

Then the lift jerked to a halt.

'Give her my love,' I said. 'Tell her I'll be round.'

'I will.'

We hesitated under the incurious eyes of the doorman, reading a magazine called *Baseball America*. The lobby's cool was welcome as water; involuntarily we paused before the blazing doorway which hung in front of us.

'So how come you're in New York?'

'Drumming up work.' He wiped his upper lip.

164

'I feel so inadequate at these meetings. American editors are robots. This one was the worst kind of hack. Said she might be able to give me a fortnightly column about being a man about town, tore apart my ideas, and then suggested we might "grab a Martini somewhere more cosy".'

'God,' I said.

I looked at him. It was on the tip of my tongue to ask if he disliked Patty, why he was so resistant to her, if he knew something I didn't – but as the words trembled on the edge of my tongue he demanded suddenly: 'Is he going to marry her?'

'Who, Mark?'

He nodded.

'I don't know.'

'No,' he said, and, leaving me no option but to follow, set off into the blazing sun.

CHAPTER 14

The infuriating thing about all this is that because I don't know when the other business began – between her and Jean-Pierre – I can't get the timings quite straight in my head. But it must have been the middle of October when I realised that Mark and Patty weren't getting along. I know it was soon after the Paddington rail crash, because the brown bunches of flowers, pile upon pile in their coloured plastic wrappings, still lay withered and rotting at the station.

By then Mark had come back from New York and Patty was virtually living with him at his new rented flat in Portland Road. I was in my garden catching up on the papers – Clinton was trumpeting his $115 billion economic surplus; he had settled with Paula Jones for his false testimony in her sexual harassment suit – when I made out Patty's voice through the kitchen window. She must have come in without me hearing the front door. 'Well, I don't think they minded,' she was exclaiming impatiently. 'She said she didn't. Oh, let's take some of those.'

'Of course she said she didn't. But the fact is she goes to huge efforts for those sorts of things.'

It was Mark David – drier than I'd heard him. Patty's tone, too, was irritated and dismissive. It was one of those insights into the way couples are behind closed doors; or, I pondered, things are beginning to sour. I wondered, turning the page, who they were talking about. One of his literary friends, no doubt. I couldn't help smiling. It would be entirely in character for Patty to agree to some do and forget about it, or turn up late, or double-book. As I had discovered to my cost, she was wildly unreliable. Just before she was due to go to wherever she was supposed to be she would have a crying fit or an argument and retreat to bed with her Poldark paperbacks and Marmite toast – much to the frustration of whoever she was meant to be meeting.

There was a pause. Then: 'Well, she doesn't *like* me,' Patty said.

'Oh, don't be ridiculous.'

'She doesn't. I heard her say so.'

'When?'

'In the toilet. Oh, not those – I don't like those.'

'But I *do*.'

Their voices faded off. I froze self-consciously. I had no wish to talk to them. Perhaps if I laid low they wouldn't know I was there. But just as I thought I had got away with it I heard a muffled exclamation. Patty threw open the door. '*Hello!* I didn't see you there! How are you!'

'Not too bad. Just sitting in the sun.'

'We're off to the park.' She wrinkled her nose. 'I've been bad. I forgot a lunch.'

'Hello, Lottie,' Mark said gravely.

'And now he's cross as two sticks. Aren't you, Mew?'

'Not now, Patty.'

'Apparently I've made a social faux – whatever. But I keep saying, she didn't mind.'

'I *said*, not now.'

This injunction seemed to have some effect: she rolled her eyes and changed the subject. 'You're so brown,' she observed. 'You know, Lottie's been to France. It sounds incredible. She stays in this place which looks like a village house from the outside, but inside it's, like, huge with a gorgeous garden and a swimming pool at the bottom. Was your dad there? Is he still bonking that twenty-year-old?'

Mark tutted. She stared. '*What?*'

'Shall we leave Lottie in peace?'

'She doesn't mind. We haven't seen each other for yonks. How's the book?'

'Endless.'

'I saw your interview with Enrique. Was he really gorgeous?'

'Very.'

'Let's have some champagne. Mew says I'm driving him crazy in Holland Park. He says he trips on my knickers every time he goes to bed.'

'*Patty.*'

168

'But I said, "It's not as if they're vibrators, or something. Everyone wears panties."'

Mark's jaw clenched. He picked up their plastic bag. 'Shall we go?'

'What?'

'I *said*, "Shall we go?"'

'What's the matter?' She frowned. 'You don't need to be so *bolshie*.'

'Then I shall go.'

He stalked from the room. The front door slammed.

We stared. 'Goodness!' I exclaimed. I burst out laughing.

But she clutched her head. 'Oh, he's driving me crazy! He's *so uptight*! I can't be one second late if I meet him, and I have to write thank you letters every minute of the day, and then he has to read them because I get them wrong – but he won't write them himself! And he sulks if I want to see my friends – he went on and on about me going to dinner at Nobu with Anton until I felt like screaming. It's like having a *jailer*, not a boyfriend.'

'Well, he's bound to be pissed off if you go out with other men.'

'It was *Anton*. It was a *restaurant review*.'

'But he fancies you!'

'He doesn't!' She frowned. 'Does he?'

'Well, well.' I smiled. 'Cup of tea?'

'Let's go to the park. Or are you working?'

I looked at my paper. I wasn't, in fact; I was

bored rigid. Suddenly the world seemed to quiver and beckon. 'Okay.'

'Goodie!' She wriggled her shoulders. 'That's another thing. He won't have junk food in the house – says the smell sticks to his hair. I mean, what kind of guy *is* he? I think he's a rabbit pretending to be a guy: all he does is nibble carrots.'

I grinned. 'Come on, you.'

Walking to the park Patty looked with interest left and right, observing the dusty streets, the blowsy roses, the men sending her approving glances. Her gaze changed when we fell behind a South African woman berating a little girl. 'You're making me shout at you in the street!' the woman yelled at the child, and she frowned, putting her hands behind her back in an undirected effort at rebellion. 'And keep up with me!' the woman ordered, hurrying on. The child resisted a moment, and then ran forlornly to catch up, her pink jelly shoes slapping the pavement.

'Foul hag,' Patty brooded. 'Why does she scream at her?'

'I suppose she doesn't know any better.'

'She should run away.'

'She's too small.'

'Well, but she should.'

She fell into musing.

'What's the matter?' I asked when we reached the park and sat down.

'I don't know.'

'If you're upset about Mark, why don't you call him?'

'I don't know.' She picked gloomily at a scab on her heel. 'He'll be cross.'

'He might not be.'

She smiled wanly. 'There are so many things I do wrong. D'you think he was like that with thingummy?'

'Christine?' I shrugged. 'Don't know.'

'It's depressing.'

'But he's a nice guy. He obviously loves you.'

'He never used to be cross though. He used to think I was amazing.'

Her phone began to ring. 'There you are,' I said. 'That'll be him. Grovelling. Wanting to take you to McDonald's.'

'Silly!' But she took it, smiling.

The sun was warm on my face but the air now had the thinner coolness of autumn. I looked at the green leaves against the blue sky and sighed. It was over a year since I had met Patty. But what had changed in my life? I still hadn't finished my book. I was still doing my interviews. I was still on and off with the copywriter.

I was sure now that he lied to me. When I rang he rarely answered the phone. Once, long before we got together, I had stood next to his then-girlfriend in a Portaloo at a wedding. She was brushing her dark hair, and met my eyes in the mirror with absolute conviction. She had said: 'He's the light of my life.'

The note of alarm in Patty's voice called me back.

'Oh, no! I'll come over.' A pause. 'Well, come here. We'll come back.'

She covered the mouthpiece. 'It's Tyrone! He's sick. Can he stay over?'

'What's wrong with his flat?'

'He's locked out. He doesn't have anywhere to go.'

I was silent. I didn't want to go home. I didn't want Tyrone in my house. I was annoyed she had invited him without asking me.

'Aren't you going back to Mark's?'

She shook her head, taking her hand off the phone. 'She says it's *fine*. Get a cab. I'll make you a hot water bottle.'

She put down the phone, plucking the grass. 'I think he's really sick.'

'Really?'

'He sounds so funny. He says he feels shivery. He just fainted at the gym.'

He arrived at my house half an hour later and I saw what she said was true: he really was sick. Tyrone never looked well at the best of times, but that day he looked like he was dying. He half-fell out of the taxi, staggered up the path, stumbled through the door and put a shaking hand to the wall. He turned his frightened eyes on Patty. 'My head hurts!'

'Oh, baby! Don't worry! I'm here.' His oversized head lolled on her shoulder as she took his suitcase.

I left them toiling up the stairs and went to answer the phone.

'It's Mark David,' I called.

'Well, I can't talk now,' Patty panted. They vanished round the stairwell.

'I see,' Mark said in a dry voice.

I had to have a drink with a friend with a dot-com who was after some money, so I left them to it. When I came back a doctor with brisk hands and a tired face was letting himself out of the front door. A pink prescription fluttered on the kitchen table; Patty was perched upstairs on a fold-up chair beside her bed. The room smelled hot and dusty. Half-full mugs and glasses stood on the floor along with an uneaten plate of toast and a festering yoghurt. I made out the bumpy outline of Tyrone by the yellow glint of the hallway light.

Patty closed the door alertly. 'He's really sick. The doctor said it might just be flu; but he wasn't one hundred per cent sure. He said to keep him quiet and make him drink fluids. He's got terrible diarrhoea.'

'What is it? Food poisoning?'

'I don't think so. He says he's only eaten tofu.'

'*Tofu?*'

She bit her thumb. 'I'd better go shopping.'

'Do you want me to go?'

'No, I'll do it. It won't take a minute.'

But when she told him she was leaving he burst into tears. So I went off to Sainsbury's –

wondering, I have to admit, if he had Aids. All that evening she sat with him; that night she slept on cushions at the foot of the bed. I felt oddly shamed by her devotion. I had no friend I would have nursed in the same way and no friend, I mused gloomily, who would have nursed me – except, perhaps, Patty.

The irony was that it seemed to begin, or hasten, the rot in her relationship with Mark David. I assumed at the time that she had begun to tire of his niceness, his wholesomeness, his steadiness: that she was too used to mean men. But it was awful to watch. She began to ignore his phone calls, bitch at him, give him orders, and vanish alone on unexplained nights out. It was a new side of her, and not a nice one. Of course she was under pressure: worried about Tyrone. I suppose in that situation Mark's calls could have seemed jealous or demanding. From my point of view, though, it was bizarre: to land a man like Mark and then drive him away. Successful, upright, wealthy, kind: what more did she want? But the one time I asked her about it she just frowned. 'He's so annoying,' she said. I think the truth was she felt trapped.

Whatever the reason, it was a shock for Mark. Such was his blazing innocence of women that Patty represented all the beauty and femininity the world could offer. He could not compute her unkindness. His voice on the phone took on a shocked, then humiliated tone. Finally one morning I heard the doorbell ring and came down to find Mark perched miserably at the kitchen table. A wedge of Cheddar glowed faintly in front of him – a propitiatory gift courtesy of the Harrods food hall, judging by the shiny white wrapping.

'You're here! Have some soup,' Patty cried when she saw me. 'It's lovely: spinach and chestnut. Mark brought it. Look: handmade.'

'Oh, I couldn't.'

'No, you must. Mustn't she, Mark?'

She was desperate not to be alone with him. Mark seemed to see it: he gave me a hollow smile. 'Absolutely.'

'Well, just quickly.' I sat down – I was ravenous. 'So how are you? How's the new play?'

'Challenging.' He sighed. He was white, and eczema reddened his eyes. 'How's the novel?'

'A nightmare. Do you find them really hard?'

'They can be. They're complicated things.'

His eyes went back to Patty and I looked at him sympathetically – I don't suppose he'd ever been in love before.

His idol was pouring out soup. 'I don't think I'm a very good nurse,' she observed blithely. 'I keep forgetting prescriptions. But we're having fun with that jigsaw. It's so hard! How do people do sky? Every piece looks the same.'

Mark wearily pinched the bridge of his nose.

'We're going to try the puzzle book this afternoon. Ty thinks he might win us some money.'

With a hiss the pan boiled over. Patty snatched it from the hob.

'Here, let me,' Mark said tiredly. He stirred it, not looking at her. 'Will you be coming over tonight?'

She bit her lip. 'Well. I promised Ty we'd watch *The Godfather*.'

'I see.'

It had begun to rain: cool fertile wetness fell through the window. I opened *The Times*. A new book was claiming that Hillary Clinton had been 'deeply in love' with Vince Foster, the deputy White House counsel. State troopers who had guarded the Governor's mansion in Arkansas claimed that Foster would turn up like 'clockwork' at the mansion when Clinton was away.

But when Foster joined the Clinton administration he became embroiled in the Nannygate, Travelgate and Whitewater scandals, and in July 1993 he was found in a wooded area near Washington, dead from a single shot to the roof of his mouth.

The *Mail* had splashed on a different story.

NEW YORK. Bill and Hillary Clinton are reported to have paid £1.3m for a house in the suburbs of Westchester. The 110-year-old Colonial-style home, with five bedrooms, a pool and a fitness room, is set in 1.1 wooded acres behind a white picket fence. Mrs Clinton needed to find somewhere to live in New York State to challenge Mayor Rudy Giuliani for the vacant Senate seat next year. Despite her liberal leanings, she chose the richest, most sought-after area in the state. Crowds gathered to gawp at the couple.

'There you go,' Mark said drily, pouring out the soup. He sat as if his knees were arthritic. 'Salt and pepper?'

Our spoons scraped the bowls.

'Autumn's coming,' I said.

'But nice to have rain,' said Patty. 'I like rain. It makes me think of rivers, and the sea, and wet leaves; and being in the country.'

'It's true,' I agreed. 'There's something soothing about rain.'

'Especially when you're in bed, all tucked up, and it's lashing at the windows.'

The church bells began to peal with graceless metallic clangs.

'What church is that?' Mark asked.

'Don't,' Patty said. 'They make me think of graveyards.'

'I fail to see what church bells have to do with graveyards.'

'They ring right next to them.'

'By that reasoning, they should equally remind you of weddings.'

'It's lovely soup,' I said.

There was silence.

'It would be nice to see you tomorrow, then,' Mark told Patty.

'Oh. Well, I might have to work.'

'Have to work? I didn't know you had a job.'

'Well, I do.'

'What kind of job?'

'A modelling job.'

'Doing what?'

'What is this – a cross-questioning?'

'I was just wondering.'

'So I might invest in a dotcom,' I said. 'It looks really good. Selling vitamins online. They think they're going to float for £15 million next year.'

'Next year?' Mark asked. 'I would be careful, in that case. The market may crash.'

'I don't think so,' I said. 'That party's just begun. The shares are zooming up.'

'Perhaps,' Mark said. 'But it's simple economics. Many of these dotcoms are half-baked. They have no prospect of making money.'

'Don't be so boring!' Patty exclaimed. She widened her eyes. 'Why are you always pouring cold water on things?'

He looked at her with stifled outrage. 'I'm merely pointing out facts.'

'Well, *don't*!'

He put his hand awkwardly through his hair.

'That was a bit harsh,' I observed, when the door closed behind him.

'But he's just so *annoying*!' Patty cried. 'He's like an old man!'

I knew better than to say anything. But privately, I gave them a month. Had I known the truth, it would have been considerably less.

In mid-October my friend Angus got married. He had been President of the Union, President of the Ball Committee, and a good mate of all of ours at university. But his love life had been disastrous until the previous year, when he had met a girl called Catrin at a dinner in Edinburgh, gone home with her that night and never left – the wedding was at a manor house in Oxfordshire, where we had all booked local B&Bs.

Mark David was taking Patty, so we had arranged to leave Tyrone in the care of his friend Erich. Then Mark ended up having to do a radio interview in London. So Patty and I went ahead on the train.

It was a soft and mellow morning, with just a slight undertow of chill to indicate the winter to come. As we stood on the platform at Paddington I remember thinking Patty looked unusually attractive. She had an air of suppressed animation – she was finally, I thought, getting over her mother.

We sat down at a table on the train with our coffees and our papers. I was just opening mine when I caught sight of Jean-Pierre and Simone through the grimy window. They were walking up the platform, unaware of anyone else, engrossed in conversation.

'Look!' I said, and waved.

Patty followed my glance. Jean-Pierre caught sight of me.

'Come here!' I mouthed. I smiled and gestured at the seat next to us, and they vanished out of sight.

'It'll be nice to see Simone,' I said. 'I hope she's okay. I'm glad she's going to the wedding. I thought she might not.'

Patty rubbed her nose.

'I know she hasn't been out much since the miscarriage,' I said. 'That was so awful.'

I looked round to see them coming into the carriage. But there was no sign of them.

'That's odd,' I said to Patty. 'They did see us, didn't they?'

'I don't know,' Patty said.

'He definitely did. Maybe they . . .' I frowned. I couldn't think of an explanation – apart from the obvious, insulting one, which was that Jean-Pierre didn't want to sit with Patty because he disliked her. But then perhaps Simone didn't feel up to chatter with a comparative stranger. 'Well,' I said, more comfortably. 'Maybe they bumped into some people.'

'Mm,' said Patty. She was staring at her *Heat* magazine. She turned the page.

'Anyway, I'm glad she came,' I said. But I felt almost rejected. I opened my *Telegraph*, and then closed it. 'I might just see if I can find them. Do you want anything?'

She shook her head.

I found them two carriages down. The train had started by then and as I lurched through the carriage door there was something about Jean-Pierre's expression that kept me from going up. He was staring out of the window with tight lips and a terrible expression. Simone was looking at him yearningly.

The moment was so clearly a bad one that I immediately turned back. But as I did so the train bucked, everyone jerked sideways and Jean-Pierre caught my eye.

His face gave a flash of irritation, instantly overlaid by welcome. He raised a hand.

'Hi!' I said, coming forward uncomfortably. 'I thought I'd see how you were.'

'Well,' Jean said. He touched his tongue to his lip. 'Well. How are you?'

'I'm okay,' I said. 'I'm with Patty. Mark's coming later. He had to do an interview.'

Simone got to her feet and kissed me on both cheeks. 'You look pretty,' she said. It was as if a flame inside her had been blown out. Her eyes were flat.

I pulled a face. 'I am *not* looking forward to this wedding. I am the last single person on the planet.'

'No, no,' Simone said. She took my hand, but her touch, normally so warm, was faint and cold.

'But how are *you*?' I said.

She shrugged.

'I'm so sorry,' I said.

'Thank you.' She smiled faintly.

'Well,' I said when the silence had stretched out. 'We're back there. If you want to visit.'

'Thanks,' Jean-Pierre said.

Simone smiled with an effort.

At our table Patty's head was bent intently over her magazine.

'They're just down the train,' I said, wrinkling my nose. 'I think they're having a row.'

'A row?' Patty asked. Her eyes fixed on me.

'Well, I don't know. Something. She's miserable. Poor thing.'

'Oh,' Patty said. She began turning the pages of the magazine in an absent way, then fell to chewing her lip.

Throughout the journey she didn't say very much. Then, a few minutes before we were due to arrive, she took her bag and disappeared to the loo. She was away so long I thought we were going to miss our stop. At last she came teetering down the carriage in her heels. Her eyes were bright and her lips were crushed-looking.

'Where have you *been*?'

'Sorry. There was such a queue!'

She began busily packing her spongebag.

Our B&B was a godforsaken place with a pink candlewick bedspread and a lopsided raffia table. We changed into our wedding outfits and took a cab to the church in a shower of hail. Jean-Pierre and Simone were there, on the far side of the altar. But it wasn't until we were milling around finding our seats at dinner that I spoke to them. Mark David had joined us by then, upright and tight-lipped in his father's morning suit, and we stopped in a ragged group by the seating plan. Simone looked miserable; Jean-Pierre hectic and uneasy. 'You're smoking!' I exclaimed as he raised a cigarette to his lips.

'I know. Bad habit.'

'I didn't know you'd started!'

His eyes flicked to Patty; then the floor.

She said: 'Can I have one?'

Simone watched as she pulled a cigarette from the packet; as he touched a lighter to the tip.

'Well, it's a lovely wedding,' I said cheerfully. 'Angus looks really happy. Mind you, he should do, it's taken long enough.'

'I think he is,' Simone said in a low voice.

I grinned. 'He thought he'd be in the Gobi forever. Did you like her dress?'

'Yes,' Simone said.

'Not as nice as yours, though.'

'You think?' She gave a sigh and looked at Jean-Pierre.

He was looking at Patty. As I watched his eyes fell and a flush rose faintly on his neck.

'I'm told there's a good Burgundy,' Mark informed Patty.

She smiled vaguely, that same concealed excitement I had noticed earlier evident in the sharp angle of her shoulder, the alert angle of her neck.

'I'm hungry. Shall we . . . ?' I said, thinking that everyone was being boringly weird, and we scattered to our tables.

My table was particularly rowdy – it held all three of Angus's younger brothers who piled into the Burgundy and exchanged boisterous anecdotes about the army and a stag the weekend before. Their good humour was so simple and uncomplicated it was contagious: by the time the cake arrived I was in fits of giggles and being teased by the oldest of the three, who, he confided in a burst of grapey confidence, planned to become a chef. I got up to go to the loo and in the entrance hall I bumped into Simone, standing by the front door. She was clutching her bag and looking out into the night as if waiting for an appointment.

'You're not going?' I asked.

She turned. 'Oh. Yes.' She wrinkled her nose. 'I'm not really having fun.'

'Oh, dear! Do you want me to come with you?'

'No!' She flapped a hand. 'How is your table?'

'Okay. Quite fun actually.' I leaned forward. 'Simone?'

'Sorry!' She wiped her eyes. 'I'm just –' She gave a ragged sigh. 'I'm an idiot!'

I stepped forward in dismay. 'Honey! What's the matter? Is it the –'

She gave a sob.

'Oh, Simone. Is it the baby?'

'It's not –' She frowned and looked away, her

face flattened into shadow. 'It's just – things are so bad at the moment.'

'Of course they are! But you'll have another.'

'I don't know.'

'You will! This is just a setback. You'll have a baby by next year.'

'Maybe.'

'Maybe? Of course!'

She shook her head. 'He's gone.'

'Who has?'

'No.' She shook her head. It was a closure of the subject: she turned, the light glinting on her brow. 'I saw the consultant,' she said. 'He said. No more children.'

'Oh, Simone. No.'

'But.' She rubbed her arms. 'It's God's will.'

I was speechless. She held my hands a minute. Then stepped back and gave a brave smile. 'But what about you? What news of the book?'

'Still going. Forever.'

'I want to read it. I want to come to your launch party.'

'You'll be guest of honour, I assure you.'

'Does the heroine die?'

'I don't know yet.'

'Don't make her die.'

Tears blurred her eyes, and she flapped her hand feebly. 'I'm not fit to be seen. I think I made Mark David worse.'

'Mark David?'

'We had a heart to heart. We're some pair.'

'I think Patty's going off him,' I said.

She nodded tiredly.

'He thinks he can't please her.'

She sighed. 'Well, no.'

She stared into the night. In the distance, over a yew hedge, a tiny pair of white lights rose and dipped toward us. The shadows streamed long and black from the statues.

'What's happening with the copywriter?'

'Not much.'

She looked behind me with sudden attention and I turned too. 'Oh, I thought you'd gone!' I exclaimed.

'How are you?' Jean-Pierre asked Simone quietly. He shoved his hands in his pockets.

'Okay. Just waiting for the cab.'

'I'm coming with you.'

'Really?'

He nodded.

'Okay.'

And her eyes met Jean-Pierre's in a kind of wistful hope.

That night I dreamed of Marrakech. The copywriter and I had gone there after we met, and that dream brought back those first few months, when there were no barriers between us, and time was a tumult, and the broken wardrobe and the stained bedside table were enchanted, and the world blossomed purple on the vine. In my dream Simone walked from the airport into the dry wind. I watched it lift her hair, caress her lips, and in front of me rose a world utterly unlike my own – scented, spiced, secretive, winding round the musky souk, the cool orange trees, the restless sand . . . the Red City –

Waking, I was flooded with that forgotten love, and yearned for it back. But when I slept again my dream had changed – now the copywriter was in a room forty floors up, and I had to unlock a lift to reach it, but whenever I tried the key a terror strangled me, and I turned and ran out of the building, my heart bursting in my ears. Then I was in the Djmaa el Fna and a snake charmer was laughing hysterically and saying over and over, 'But he loves her – she loves *her*!'

I snapped on the light and the room sprang up, stable with light. It was four in the morning, and before I could think better of it I rang the copywriter, breathing shallowly on the line. He answered it on first ring.

'Hello.'

'Are you at home?'

'Yes. I thought you were at Angus's wedding.'

'I am. Why are you up?'

'You just rang.'

'But why were you awake?'

'It's a little hard to sleep through a mobile phone.'

'But you were awake anyway. What were you doing, at four in the morning?'

'Lottie, did you actually want something?'

'I had a bad dream.'

'Did you? Hang on. Let me go into the kitchen.'

I heard a muffled creaking, then a girl's voice, faint, in the background.

'Who was that?'

'Who was what?'

'Are you *with* someone?'

'Don't be ridiculous.'

'You are! Aren't you?'

'Lottie, must we always have an argument?'

I put down the phone.

CHAPTER 15

We got back to London to find Erich running down the stairs and Tyrone being carried in a wheelchair into an ambulance. In hospital they diagnosed malaria, of all things – he had been on holiday to Sierra Leone two years before.

He came out at the start of November, far too weak to look after himself. So the box room in the attic, which still had my aunt's frayed red and green hardbacks on the shelves, became the focus of the house. Patty spent all her time up there, when she wasn't at modelling jobs or auditions. She and Tyrone whiled away the dark winter afternoons doing jigsaws, drawing pictures and writing poems. I still have one of Patty's I found there after she had gone: '*Life/ I am of both your directions/ Somehow remaining, / Hanging downward the most, / Strong as a cobweb in the wind, / Existing more with the cold frost . . .*'

During the short darkening days they would spend entire days chatting in the calm voices of people completely comfortable with each other. I generally couldn't hear what they were saying. But

189

one afternoon, after I had fallen asleep on my bed, I woke to the rumble of a sash window and Patty's voice above me. As my window was open, it floated down to me quite clearly.

'. . . want to be really wonderful, you know? I know that sounds stupid, but I do. I want to be a really, really good actress, and it makes me nearly crazy – because I'm trying to get the truest part of me out. Sometimes I think, "All I need to be is true." But it's so hard. Because of the shame. And that's what he understands. Because he's sort of bent double with it.'

'What's *he* so ashamed of?'

'I don't know. His family, I think. I feel so bad for him. He's miserable. He's all tied up in knots. The night we got together he said, "You're the saddest girl I've ever met and I'm the guiltiest man." We were watching the sun come up. And I remember seeing a black cat jump up on a wall and thinking, "The funny thing is I've never felt so happy in my life."'

'That's how I felt with Otto.'

'Oh, Otto was lovely.'

'So what are you going to do about Mark?'

I frowned. Mark? Hadn't she been talking about Mark?

'I don't know.' She must have wandered to the window, because her sigh fell a storey. 'I'm sorry for him. He doesn't know how to live.'

'He doesn't know how to do a lot of things.'

A giggle. 'You know she left me a message?'

'What, another one?'

'Oh. I told you.'

'Yes, that was sick.'

'It was, wasn't it?'

The bed creaked. 'See, what it is,' Patty went on, more faintly, 'is that I'm not in a life of my own. You know that feeling? Like when you were with Otto. It's like: he likes me in bed, but he doesn't like the rest of me. He wants me to be as buttoned-up as he is. It's suffocating. Last night I had this dream that I was being smothered by honey: a wave of it was oozing over me and I was choking.'

'Ooh: that's *very* Freudian.'

'Is it? Why?'

'That's cum. That's like your velvet dream.'

'That was after the letter, though.'

'Yes, and I still think you should have said something about that.'

'What, like, "I read in your letter to your sister that you thought I was an angel. Now you think I'm a succubus who steals your talent and sucks up all your energy. What the fuck were you doing leaving that shit out for me to read?"'

'He should suck *his* bus.'

Another giggle. Another creak. 'Let's have lunch.'

'What shall we have?'

'That ham. That bread.'

'Is she here?'

'Don't think so.'

'She's definitely pissed off with me.'

'Is she? Why?'

'She hates me being here.'

'She hasn't said so. She doesn't.'

'I bet she does, though. I bet *she*'s never had an orgasm.'

'D'you think?'

'Oh God, yes. She's so inhibited. She's like the ultimate victim.'

'No, she's really nice. She's really kind.'

'Nice, I grant you. But controlling. And kind of weird. Fancy having all that money and so little fun. And have you noticed she never makes eye contact when she talks? She's like totally disconnected.'

'Do you think?'

'Totally.'

'That's how I feel half the time.'

'Yes, darling, but you're normal.'

I stood sharply. Let myself out of the house.

That year the winter roared in with a series of wrenching storms. As if in sympathy, my life, too, began to crumble into pieces.

The first thing to go was the copywriter and me. I mean, for good, finally. I don't know if I've mentioned that friends had been saying to me, for months, even years, that they had seen him with other women. But whenever I asked him about it he would deny it, and seem so amazed, and offended, that I would let it drop. But several things finally pierced my denial. The girl's voice I heard in the background when I called him from the wedding was one. Next I found out that he had been lying about his family. He had told me when we met that his uncle had a title. Then I sat next to a man with that very title at a wedding. 'You've been led up the garden path, young lady,' he declared, with a pitying look in his eye.

Finally I bumped into a school friend at a christening, vast in a pink Whistles dress. We were chatting outside the church when I mentioned that I had been with the copywriter to Sicily.

She fixed me with a look. 'You do know,' she said, 'that he's *living* with Tiffany Boden.'

I told her he wasn't.

'They're *living*,' she repeated – she obviously thought I was completely mad – 'in Edwardes *Square*. I've *seen* them. I've been there to *dinner*.'

'That's absurd,' I said. 'Do you think I wouldn't know?'

I'll spare you the details. To sum up, my school friend emailed me the address. I climbed down their basement steps and looked into the bedroom. He obviously was there, because a pair of his cufflinks were scattered on the windowsill. One of the cashmere jumpers I had given him at Christmas was lying on the bed. On top of it, like a metaphor for our relationship, was a blue Nicole Farhi dress that, ironically, I had recently bought myself.

He denied it, of course. When he finally came clean we had a rather difficult scene. I cut up his clothes and left them on her doorstep. And that was the end of the copywriter.

CHAPTER 16

That first time I saw them together was pure chance.

It was late that November, the sky high blue, the roses pink in the pale winter sun. Coming down Artesian Road I saw Patty ahead of me turning into a pub, by our house, called the Cock and Bottle. 'Patty!' I called. But she didn't hear me. She entered the pub.

I ran after her smiling and opened the door. But she wasn't there. I frowned. Then I put my head into the back room. It was empty apart from a man at the far end sitting with his back to me. I only clicked who it was as I was turning away.

Patty had been going out with Mark David more than four months by then. I remember thinking they must be in the loo. Well, I'm not sure what I thought. I just ran forward and did a playful jump onto Jean-Pierre's shoulders. He reached back and wound his hands round my legs. He said: 'You can't want *another* fuck.'

At which I laughed in amazement – I had never heard him talk like that before. And then he turned. 'Oh my God,' he said. 'Lottie.'

He seemed absolutely horror-struck. This made me laugh, because, after all, it wasn't a big deal. 'Filthy!' I said, smiling. 'Where's Simone?' I sat down.

He didn't reply.

'Jean?' I said.

Then I saw the green woollen bag lying by the ashtray. It was the one Patty had had with her the first day I met her, in LA.

I said: 'Is Patty here?'

It was a casual question, but Jean-Pierre seemed almost scared.

'We're just having a drink,' he said.

'I know!' I smiled. 'Where's Simone?'

Jean-Pierre glanced behind me and I saw Patty coming from the door to the loo. She was walking fast, with her head up, and she had a triumph about her. It's hard to explain. The closest I can come is the kind of certainty she had the day I first saw her coming into Beverly Hills Hotel pool. As if all her nerve-ends were connected and were smouldering.

She saw me and put a hand to her mouth.

I smiled. 'Didn't you hear me calling? I was right behind you.'

Patty looked at Jean-Pierre. He crushed out his cigarette. He said: 'Lottie just came in.'

Patty stood a moment as if unsure what to do. She pulled out a stool and sat down.

'So how was the audition?' I asked.

'Oh. Good,' she said.

'Good?' I echoed. I couldn't understand the atmosphere. 'Are you with Mark?'

It was then I took in what Patty was wearing. She was in a black gypsy skirt and red jumper and she had a doodle on her hand. It was in blue Biro that had jolted across the skin. I remember reading it in slow motion: 'JP 4 PB'.

I stared at Jean-Pierre. He looked into the distance – his face set like chalk.

I said: 'What's going on?'

Patty quivered. Her face pinched.

I frowned. I stared at Jean-Pierre. 'Jean?'

'I didn't *mean* to!' Patty burst out. She reached for the cigarettes with a shaking hand. Jean-Pierre put his head in his hands. A wave of anger ripped through me.

'What the fuck do you think you're doing?'

'We love each other,' Patty said in a quavering voice.

I stared at them in disbelief. 'How long has this been going on?'

Patty refused to meet my eye. Jean-Pierre put his hand to his face.

I was shaking with anger. 'I can't believe you would do this.' I felt tears in my eyes. 'I can't *believe* it!' I repeated.

Jean-Pierre licked his lips. 'It's not what you think,' he said in a low voice. 'It's not something I –'

'Is that J-P?' an Australian voice interrupted, rising on an excited note of joy. 'It sodding well

197

is! How's it going, cobber? It's been too fuckin' long!'

Jean-Pierre looked up. 'Vinnie,' he said weakly.

'You little bastard! Still soakin' when you should be at work?'

He was a tattooed Australian with hair bleached short, like a nailbrush. He beamed his delighted grin on Patty. 'This her?'

'Oh – no – this is a friend.'

'Bad luck!' He laughed raucously. 'No offence meant! Thought you were the missus. I'm Vin.'

He stuck out a huge paint-spotted hand.

Patty took it faintly. 'Patty.'

'Thrilled to meet ya!' He stood back, grinning delightedly. 'So when was it? 1995? The Boquitas Pintadas!'

'Right.'

'Remember the barmaid? You know who she married?'

Finally he perceived he had come at a bad time. 'Well,' he said, his innocent eyes fading. 'I'll leave you to it.'

'Yes. Sorry. Not a good time.'

'Just don't leave it another ten years, hey!'

I said: 'I'm off.'

Patty found my eye. Her upper lip was jerking in a convulsive tic. 'Are you really cross?'

'You disgust me,' I said.

Rage propelled me from the pub. I stepped in front of a car, dizzy with betrayal. Had Simone known at the wedding – was that why she left so

198

early? Was that why Mark was so down? When did it start? Not in New *York*?

I was at the house when Jean-Pierre caught me. He grabbed me, panting. 'Lottie. *Wait* a minute!'

'Leave me alone!'

'I need to talk to you!'

I threw him off. 'Fuck off and die!'

His temper cracked. 'For God's sake, stop!'

'What about *Simone*?'

'Do you think I don't care?' His eyes flared. 'Do you think I haven't thought about that?'

'*And?*'

He flexed his hands in an effort at self-control. A Volvo nuzzled us, predatory, stalking the kerb at our feet. 'Can we go inside?'

'No.'

'Open the door.'

He followed me into the kitchen.

'Well?'

But to my surprise he now had a neutral, almost distant expression. 'I haven't told you about my father,' he said, and I still remember the way he said it, not: 'I don't think I've told you about my father,' but the certainty of it: 'I haven't told you about my father.' He looked straight at me. 'He was psychotic. He hanged himself when I was three.'

His face was smooth as if it had been washed by a great wave.

He said: 'That's why I never wanted children. I didn't want my children to go mad.'

I frowned. 'But they wouldn't – surely.'

199

'They might. It can be heritable.' He swallowed. 'I wouldn't do that to Simone.'

'Do what? But – she was pregnant.'

'And lost the baby.'

I felt suddenly scared. 'But – that wasn't –'

He shot me a contemptuous stare. 'Of course not. But the point is I didn't tell her. I hadn't *told* her! And now she can't have any more she's – Jesus, I'm a curse. I am a fucking curse!'

I suddenly saw that he believed he had doomed the baby; that his fears had caused the miscarriage. It was a crack showing me for the first time the turmoil so carefully guarded and I was moved. That he hadn't even told Simone! I glimpsed the extent of his defences, the depth of his vulnerability. I felt an electric current between us. I seized his hands. 'You're not! You're wonderful! Honestly!'

'Oh, spare me.'

'No, really! You're just upset – and confused – and amazing.' I said in a whisper: 'You're the most amazing person I know.'

'Knock, knock,' said a voice, and Tyrone appeared in the doorway. He eyed us with interest. Jean-Pierre dropped my hands and wearily rubbed his face.

'Hello, Tyrone,' I said.

'Hello.' He widened his eyes. 'Sorry. I'll pop back later!' Elaborately, he shut the door.

I took Jean-Pierre's hands again. 'So what are you going to do?' He shook his head.

'You know you can't carry on.'

The doorknob rattled. 'Sorry,' Tyrone mouthed. 'Just wanted this.' He took up his mobile with exaggerated care. The door closed shut and I looked into Jean-Pierre's eyes.

'You know you can't carry on.'

Steps came up the path and the door reopened. Patty stood in the doorway. Her eyes were huge and her chest was rising and falling.

'Jean?' she breathed.

He sighed. 'Patty.'

'What's going on?'

He put up his hands. 'I have to go.'

'I'm coming with you!'

He shook his head. 'Look, I'll call you later.'

He paused in front of her, not looking at her; fearfully she clutched his arm. 'Jean?'

'I have to go.'

She gave a terrified sob. 'No!'

'Darling –'

'No! Please don't! Leave *her*! Don't leave me!'

He shook her off. 'I have to *go*.'

She was shivering all over. 'When will you call?'

He gave her a look. Its meaning was unreadable: he would call, or not call – it was impossible to say. The front door banged and I jerked open the dishwasher. I was so angry I could hardly speak. I said: 'I think you'd better go.'

I took two glasses out of the dishwasher and thrust them away. She said behind me, on a sob: 'Lottie?'

I turned. 'Did you hear me?'

She began weeping, a tempest of tears. 'But we didn't mean it to happen! We tried to stop it, but we couldn't, it was –'

But I wouldn't listen. I had no sympathy for her that day. Her joyful promise had finally been exposed as counterfeit, and my love for her had vanished.

Tyrone came into the kitchen. 'What's going on?'

'You'd better ask Patty.'

He stared at me as if he was trying to understand something very important in a foreign language.

I went into the garden and began pulling up weeds. For the next hour muffled thuds and creaks issued from the house. Then the distant purr of an engine, a ring at the bell, and a slam. When I went inside the rooms were empty. Silence reigned.

CHAPTER 17

The leaves on my maple turned the orange of bonfires that winter. A mist faint as cow parsley hung on the yellow spikes of grass. The air lost its bracing nip of new beginnings as the moon sank beneath the fence like a balloon. The paper said the colours of the leaves were the most beautiful in living memory. They fell, lime-yellow, red-green, orange-brown, landing with a silent splash. Blackberries shrivelled on the traffic-dirtied hedgerows, and the sunshine, when it came, was sidelong and nostalgic.

I had begun to learn to dance. Every Monday I drove through the bitter dark to a church hall in Marylebone to waltz with a policeman who tried to manipulate me with humourless calm. 'Stop jigging!' he would exclaim, as the couple practising their wedding dance shuffled a solemn circle.

I was trying to fill up my time. Without Patty or the copywriter the evenings were endless. I knew I was doing the right thing. But I had to remind myself of it again and again that winter, when the house seemed so empty, and I realised how much Patty had worked her way into my life.

She sent me a letter maybe a week after she had left. I knew it was from her right away. It was in a small grey envelope, grubby and dog-eared at the corner. She had written it in pencil and two different kinds of pen, and the script zigzagged up and down the lined paper, wandering up the margins as if in a maze.

I know you were upset I didn't tell you, I meant too, I was frightened you wouldnt understand but I just couldnt help it, it was like a hurricane it just came over me I couldn't stop it, you know what it was like becose of your husband and I hope you can forgive me becos you know what its like to suffer as well and I now your upset about Mark but he was just never the same as me and I never made him happy and Jean is, he knows about skewers through your soul. I read once about Freda Karlo the south American painter, she was on a bus and a handrail went through her and gold paint spilt over her and that's how it feels to be me I think men like the gold outside of me but they dont want the inside except jean does, hes the only man who understands it. But I am in dire straight's right now. I have thought of ending it all because hes the love of my life and I need him so much. But I sware I never meant to hurt you. I never wanted to –

My God: she was pathetic! I hurled it at the fire.

Those nights I sat by the fire compulsively reading my psychology books, learning terms like *separation theory* and *individuation* and *parentification*. I went to bed at nine pm and I would still be there at ten the next morning. Sometimes the scrape of the cleaner's key would force me into clothes; my blood was like lead as I sat over my paper in the coffee shop. It was the peak of the dotcom boom. I read about my college friends making millions. Everyone was leaving jobs and starting businesses, hightailing it to a dazzling future.

BUY, buy, buy. In the past six weeks a feeding frenzy of share-buying by private investors has erupted. Investors are besieging share dealing services, jamming telephone lines and seizing up the Internet. Stockbrokers are struggling to cope as their systems threaten to melt down under the extraordinary demand. Many of the new breed of investors looking to make a quick killing have been left fuming after being unable to trade.

Investors' imagination has been fired by internet and telecoms shares. They crave Vodafone, BATM, Scoot.com and the penny shares of companies such as Pacific Media and Medi@invest. For any company with .com in its name, private investor interest rises tenfold.

The City, which had expected a gradual wind-down for Christmas, has never seen anything like it. Traders complain they have been shackled to their desks. Pubs normally packed before Christmas are almost deserted at lunchtime.

'It is completely mad. It is the modern day creation of a gold rush. Everyone wants a piece of the action,' says Richard Hunter, head of dealing at NatWest Stockbrokers. The dramatic surge in activity has seen daily trading volumes on the London Stock Exchange explode from 60,000 in October to more than 140,000 earlier this month.

Brokers say the demand is being driven by private investors who have signed up to an Internet dealing service. Charles Schwab, Britain's biggest Internet share-dealing service, handled 12,500 trades on Monday, up from just 6,000 two months ago. Rivals such as Barclays Stockbrokers, NatWest Stockbrokers, Dealwise, Stocktrade and E*Trade all report a doubling in demand. The number of active private investors has risen from 250,000 just two months ago to more than 400,000.

Some of the share price increases have been truly mind-boggling. The shares of Durlacher, the Internet investment company, are 69 times as high as they were a year ago. Infobank, which connects companies with online suppliers, is 42 times higher, while BATM, which has clever switching technology, has seen its shares surge by more than 20 times this year.

'The proliferation of investment magazines, web sites and television programmes such as Channel 4's Show Me the Money has enticed ever more people to become investment addicts. Some brokers say the market is being driven by 'fear, greed and ignorance'. It is littered with anecdotes of investors who do not care about the price, know nothing about the company they want to buy and have no interest in the financial data. They just want the stock.

Robbie Crawford, a 29-year-old inventor and computer consultant from Bonnyrigg, Midiothian, admits that he has become addicted since he started trading over the Internet in February. He started with £16,000 and has seen the value of his shares swing violently. Triumphs have included making £3,500 in one day on imagination Technologies and a £6,000 profit on Pacific Media. I get bored after a while and switch to other stocks. My £16,000 is my break point – as long as I can keep above that I am happy.'

I had just come back from a particularly grisly date at Kensington Place when the phone went.

'I'm calling with an invite,' said Simone.

I switched on the lamp, startled. Simone. I had not seen her since she had told me she couldn't have children. And since I had seen Patty and Jean-Pierre. I thought of his expression, stripped like a bone, as he spoke about his father. Patty's terrified eyes.

'Oh, *hi*!' I said.

'Are you okay?'

'Yes! Well, no. I've just had a date.'

'A date!' Her voice deepened with enthusiasm. None of my friends had liked the copywriter; they were all hopeful I would find someone else. 'How was it?'

'Shocking. I called him a womaniser.'

'Is he?'

'Oh, I don't know. Probably not. Then I insisted on paying.'

'Oh.'

'I know. But why should they pay, if I can?'

'Because they like to. To look after you.'

I felt a pang of despair – at Jean-Pierre's betrayal, at Simone's childlessness, at my loneliness, a problem, it seemed, I could never solve. 'Oh, God! How are things with you?'

'Don't ask.'

'What a pair!' I sniffed, laughing. 'When am I going to see you?'

'On Thursday. I want to take you to a party.'

'A party? Whose?'

'Anton Lord's. He's launching a dotcom.'

'Oh. Gosh. I don't know. We're not exactly friends.'

'But I want to get out of the house.'

I thought of Jean-Pierre. 'I'm not sure.'

'Please. I want to see you. So does Jean.'

So he hadn't told her. My heart skipped a beat. 'How is he?'

'Oh, you know. Quiet.'

I bet he is, I thought. 'Well, let me check my diary. Hang on.' I got it out of my bag. Stopped. Mark David and Patty wouldn't be going – would they? 'Will there be dozens of people?'

'I don't think so. Mark was invited' I held a breath 'but he doesn't think he can make it.'

We talked on, and by the time the conversation ended it was clear that she was expecting me to go.

The minute I put down the phone it rang again.

'Hello,' said Jean-Pierre.

My heart thumped. 'Hi!'

'How are you?'

'Okay. How are you?'

'Okay.' A pause. 'We need to talk.'

'Okay.'

'Can we meet?'

'Okay.'

'When are you free?'

'Um. Next week?'

'Wednesday?'

'Okay.'

I put down the phone. His voice called up the thick curves of his cheek, his lips.

★   ★   ★

209

In those days I went to a doctor on Westbourne Grove. It was there, in a tattered copy of the *Economist*, that I came on the piece about Kaplan. It was dated July 25 1999 – four months before.

The small black and white picture showed Ed Kaplan stalking down a flight of white steps framed by palm trees, a sign behind him announcing 'Beverly Hills Police Department', his hand raised as if warding something away. Behind him wavered the thin, frightened figure of a woman. She had delicate features and big smudgy eyes. Her heavily set hair had come askew and by some trick of a paparazzo's shutter her scarf was blowing out in the shape of a cross. '*Ed Kaplan and his wife Betsey,*' read the caption.

STRANGE GOINGS ON IN BRENTWOOD

Even those accustomed to the twists of Californian politics have been surprised this week. After a 17-month FBI sting, federal prosecutors charged the real estate developer and political fundraiser Ed Kaplan with conspiracy, obstruction of justice and interstate promotion of prostitution. The bureau, not usually known for its sense of humour, named the investigation Operation I Love You California after the official state song.

The move came as a shock. Kaplan has connections at the highest level. He has made more than $1.5m (£825,000) in political contributions.

Agents began investigating Kaplan for violations of federal tax and fraud statutes and for purported violation of federal campaign contribution laws in February 1998. The evidence against him was provided by two witnesses – a married couple described as close associates of Kaplan. Kaplan allegedly initiated 'a scheme to orchestrate a covert videotaped seduction' of John Pozzi, the male witness, in an attempt to thwart the investigation.

In other words, according to the FBI, Kaplan recruited a party girl known as Meena Saragoussi – with whom he was himself having an extra-marital affair – to have sex with Pozzi. The videotape was later sent to Pozzi's wife Hilly, the other cooperating witness in the investigation.

But L. Lin Scott, Kaplan's attorney, said that the charges were baseless. 'Ed Kaplan is one of the most respected business leaders in the community and widely known as a very generous philanthropist. The charges are entirely baseless. Mr Kaplan is confident that once the facts are fully disclosed in a courtroom he will be completely exonerated.'

Kaplan posted $2m (£1.1m) bail in federal court in Los Angeles, California but made no comment outside the courthouse, where he appeared with his wife Betsey.

While the political community has been startled by the allegations, they are not a complete surprise. The FEC fined Kaplan $500,000 (£275,000) last year for improperly contributing money to the campaigns of several prominent Democrats. A White House spokeswoman, Annalee Ellis said she had no comment on the charges.

In a further twist Kaplan is suing the *Washington Post* columnist Paul Safire. He says that Safire libelled him in broadcast and newspaper interviews over both the Saragoussi affair and last year's 'Smoking Gun' scandal.

'Lottie Wakefield?' the doctor called. I screwed up the magazine and put it in my bag. Meena Saragoussi, it developed, as I finished the piece later in my kitchen, had worked for an escort agency.

One of Kaplan's allegations is that Safire named him as a guest at the notorious 'Smoking Gun' New Year's Eve party at the Amaryllis nightclub on Sunset Boulevard in Los Angeles. The body of the cosmetics heiress Ellie Tallit was found dead in the ground floor toilets. Several members of certain Arab countries' embassies were arrested along with numerous models and party girls, including Saragoussi. Police also seized several grammes of heroin and cocaine.

Safire later admitted Kaplan had not been present. But he did not back down entirely. 'I don't think [Kaplan] had anything to do with [Tallit],' he said. 'But I think he could have known it was going to happen.'

The problem is that while it is understandable that Kaplan is aggrieved and angry at this libel, it is doubtful he will be able to base a successful case upon it. One reason is that Safire is not only a respected journalist, but a sympathetic defendant. He is the father of a murdered schoolboy who has, despite his grief, campaigned for justice for the families of other murder victims. Kaplan meanwhile has had several brushes with the law and has not been entirely candid during the FBI investigation. He failed to provide information about Tallit that could have contributed to the arrest of her assailants. His behaviour gave other grounds of suspicion – he disposed of a Franck Muller watch he'd kept in his office in an out-of-town skip and released schedules of his whereabouts that later were shown to be inaccurate. Police sources have claimed that Kaplan had once been close to Tallit.

No doubt he was partly trying to protect his marriage to former Georgia beauty queen and childhood sweetheart Betsey Blaine. The couple's two daughters gained some profile after they danced with President Clinton at a Democrat fundraiser two years ago.

'My client has nothing to be guilty about,' Scott maintained in a statement last week. If he is wrong, the case could open a Pandora's box that reaches as far as the White House.

I frowned. So . . . was Kaplan involved in the Smoking Gun scandal? Or not? What exactly had happened to Ellie Tallit? It was clear he was at the very least a rogue. I went back to the beginning. I was halfway through when the window rattled and I froze with a foolish fear: Kaplan!

It was Tyrone.

'Morning,' he mouthed, and stuck his face to the window. He was in a zip-up blue cardigan, his fine hair teased into a perky attempt at a Mohican.

I opened the window. 'Excuse me – what are you doing?'

He pulled a naughty face. 'Hello.'

'Were you trying to break in?'

'Well. Only a tiny bit.' He eyed the window. 'I *think* I could have got it open, though I'm a bit weak, since my illness-enforced diet.'

'Tyrone, what do you want?'

'Oh, I'm fine, thanks. Much better.' He eyed the window opening. 'I know I've lost weight but this is ridiculous. Will you open the door?'

'What do you want?'

He sauntered past me into the kitchen. 'It looks different. Have you painted it?'

'No.'

'It looks darker.' He saw my expression. 'I have a question.'

I sighed. 'Well?'

'Who do I take to Sleaze?'

'To what?'

'To Sleaze. It's the gay millennium party in Ibiza.' He tripped to the table and sat down. 'See, all my party friends have disappeared to Aids or long-term relationships. I did think about Otto, but he's being forced to hover over mainframes in case they blow up. Y2K – so tiresome.'

He picked up the article and examined it. I took it from him. He grinned. 'So I *think* I'm going to ask this boy I've been looking at for months at the gym. Because I *think* he's been looking at me. We exchange glances in the mirror. Sometimes, when I go past, we smile.'

'So why don't you?'

'Well, we haven't talked yet. And he *might* not fancy me. But I'm fairly sure he does. I don't think this is just being friendly to a fellow early morning gym person. This morning we nearly spoke.'

'So ask him.'

He tossed his leg up on his knee. 'Well, he *may* have commitment problems. He may be a bit young.' He looked round. 'Can I have some of that cheese?'

'No.'

'You are mean. Of course it's totally *verboten*. Since I've been in hospital, you know, my tongue diagnostics are transformed. I have *no* heat on my liver. According to my therapist I've undergone the equivalent of an extreme detox. She's *thrilled* I'm now banned only from shellfish, dairy, red meat and alcohol. So last night, showing a remarkable level of restraint, I had, sequentially, shellfish, Mongolian lamb, a laksa thing with duck, and a glass of Sauvignon.' He stuck out his tongue. 'Can you see?'

'Tyrone, what do you want?'

He stuck it in. 'Patty's miserable.'

I stared. 'Is that why you came?'

'I thought you could bury the hatchet.'

'Are you completely mad?'

'Hm?' He raised his eyebrows.

'Are you unaware of what she's done?'

He frowned. 'Don't think so. Didn't she fall in love?'

I felt the anger rise. 'With a married man! Who happens to be married to one of my best friends!'

'Jean-Pierre, you mean. Well. He's not exactly whiter than white.'

'What's that supposed to mean?'

He shrugged. 'What he gets up to. I've seen him. At Soho House.'

'Since he's been married?'

'Over the years.'

'So not since he's been married.'

He folded his arms and smiled consideringly. 'I love being in love. But I'm not sure I'd fancy it again. When I met Otto I was like a madman. If he'd have asked me to rob a bank I'd have done it. Crash a car . . . I *did* crash a car. Though admittedly that wasn't deliberate.'

'Will you get to the point?'

He didn't seem to hear. 'So if Patty . . . burned down my flat. Or slept with Erich. Well, she did sleep with Erich. Of course you're cross. But that's life. People do things. You can't cut them off because they aren't always what you want.'

I gave a hysterical laugh. 'So it's fine if they sleep with your husband?'

Tyrone examined his nail. 'I didn't think you were married to him.' He dug his tongue into a tooth. 'My mother had an affair. With the milkman, would you believe. She and my dad are happy as Larry now.'

I crossed my legs. 'Well, bully for them. But frankly I'm not going to kiss and make up because Patty has decided she's upset about losing her nice place to live and it's made her life a little bit difficult. I'm rather old-fashioned, you see. I don't believe in adultery. And I don't believe you can act exactly how you want, when you want. And frankly I don't want to see her ever again. And now, if you don't mind, I've got some work to do.'

'I know,' Tyrone said, and to my surprise he smiled – a warm, comforting smile that made me wonder if I'd misjudged him all along. 'I've got to too. I *think* I'm at the beginning of a cold. Of course it's self-inflicted. Everyone at the salon said I shouldn't come in and spread my germs. What I couldn't tell them was that germs were *not* the cause of my current plight. But then a full description of what is is probably outside the bounds of acceptable discussion in a hairdresser's.'

'Perhaps I should tell you,' I said coolly, 'that Patty's ex is in trouble. With the police.'

'And there'll be more where *that* came from,' Tyrone said mysteriously. He ran his tongue smugly over his front teeth. 'Now, all I need is my "Heterosexually Challenged" shirt.'

He disappeared into the laundry room. 'I like to wear it on flights,' he called, his voice muffled. 'I like to think it wards off one of my pet hates, which is the man in front of me reclining into my lap. Every time I fly I get stuck behind a man who just *has* to put his chair back. When I went to Ibiza I was behind this *foul* little person. He was fat, he was horrible to the stewardesses and worst of all he was ugly. To add to my woes, he *arrogantly* put his chair back. No graceful decline. Oh, no. A huge whack on my knees. So I started to kick the back of his seat. Then I slammed the tray table shut a few times. That got his attention. He peered round and Erich and I fell about laughing. "Sorry!" I said. "Mistake!"'

CHAPTER 18

The memory of my meeting with Jean-Pierre is not one I want to rehearse. We met on a rainy morning late in November, the day after Tina Brown had thrown what the *Telegraph* said was the defining party of the century, to launch *Talk*, her new magazine. She gave it on Liberty Island in New York, with Gwyneth Paltrow in dominatrix leather, and Robert de Niro celebrating his divorce, his arm draped around supermodels. Madonna drank cocktails with Lauren Bacall and the first issue ran an interview with Hillary Clinton about Clinton's womanising, which she claimed was the result of the abuse he had suffered as a child.

Some columnists said it was the best party since Truman Capote's Black and White Ball. Others claimed hubris was thick in the air as the celebrities looked at Manhattan over the dark glittering water. And so it proved, three years later, when Brown, sobbing, closed the magazine after the Twin Towers collapsed. But that day it seemed to stand for everything dazzling and hopeful: the brave new world offering fortunes for the taking, with only the end of the millennium to lend a balancing darkness to the midday sun.

In that first issue, later, I would read a grimmer account of the era. It was an article about people with borderline personality disorder – such as Princess Diana and Marilyn Monroe, according to the writer, a New York psychiatrist. He said it was a mental illness characterised by intense, unstable relationships, hypersensitivity, self-destructiveness, depression, manipulativeness and demandingness, plus black and white thinking and frantic efforts to escape abandonment. The whole Western world, he theorised, had become so paranoid and unstable that it could itself be diagnosed as borderline.

I think in the end this was Patty's affliction. But in some ways it applied to all of us during that millennial gold rush, when hopes rode bareback, and dreams existed to be speared.

I didn't have my chat with Jean-Pierre in London. We did it in Blenheim, of all places. I had been commissioned to write about its revamp for *Tatler*; he was flying to Beirut the next day. So he came with me to Woodstock.

I had bought a new Volvo, and when I picked him up in Oxford he hunched awkwardly beside me, the seat tilted too far back. He had a thick red spot under his ear, and his skin smelled of bed. I was self-conscious, acutely aware of my profile and the eczema under my eye.

221

'Nice motor.'

'Thanks.'

He struggled to sit upright. We drove past a man selling tight bunches of roses. 'RED ROSES,' the sign declared, and the word 'red' had crimson drops dripping cartoonishly.

'No traffic,' I remarked.

'No. It's usually clear in the morning.'

We drove in silence.

'So how are things?' he asked heavily.

'Not too bad. I'm learning to dance . . . How are you?'

'I'm taking that column.'

'Which column?'

'The man about town one. With the editor I met in New York. She says first-person pieces are the next big thing.'

'But you can't do that!'

He gave a bitter snort. 'We need the cash.'

It began to rain. The windscreen wipers, I discovered, didn't work properly.

'I'm sorry,' he said at last, 'about the other day.'

I pushed back my hair. 'That's okay.'

'I never wanted to involve you.'

I wondered what exactly he meant. 'No.'

'Watch it!'

I braked just in time to avoid the lorry.

'Sorry.'

I said, after a minute: 'I haven't told anyone. What you said about your father.'

He gave a nod. 'Thanks.'

'How's Simone?'

'She's okay.'

We fell silent again.

Outside Oxford he cleared his throat. He said: 'I gather you told Patty to move out.'

'Did she tell you that?'

He nodded.

'Obviously.'

He looked out of the window. At last I said: 'Did you read the Hillary Clinton interview?' Then realised, too late, the implications.

'Clinton,' Jean-Pierre said contemptuously, and shook his head.

Woodstock rose in front of us: grey, stone-fronted. We drove past a tantalising alley and several low-browed teashops, and pulled up at the entrance to Blenheim. Two guards raised their heads from a golfing magazine. 'You're in luck. Press is free. Straight down the drive. Car park on the left.'

The house grew on the green slope. Its gates gleamed gold.

'Very nice,' said Jean-Pierre. 'Queen Anne's bounty, wasn't it? To Marlborough.'

In the car park the rain spread puddles and an earthy smell. A shaft of sun pierced the blue cloud. 'I'll mooch here while you do your stuff,' Jean-Pierre said. He looked at me. 'Then we'll talk.'

My heart gave a thump. Was he leaving Simone for Patty? It wasn't possible. I thought if he didn't tell me he was going to stop seeing her, I would tell him I would tell Simone. This thought made my stomach fizz and I stepped into a puddle, soaking my shoe. It squelched for the next hour as I trailed the museum gloom of the house, under the dusty tapestries and the portraits of dead children.

When I came back into the courtyard I felt a sudden thrill of pride. Jean-Pierre was leaning at the foot of the steps and people were glancing at him curiously – at his casual good-looking glamour. When he saw me he stretched.

'I'm hungry,' I told him.

'Then we must give you food.'

'Oh, please not frogs' legs.'

'We had those at school,' he said. 'With lizards' eyes.'

'Your school!'

People looked after us as we crossed the court-yard and I felt suddenly happy. 'Rather a nice way,' I said, tossing my hair, 'to earn some money.'

The restaurant was in the basement of the building. The cellar smell took me back to the Magdalen cloisters. The windows framed views of mossy statues and black wheelie bins crawling with wasps. 'We're about to close,' the waitress said. She slapped through a swing door.

Jean-Pierre raised his eyebrows.

I said: 'There is a café, I think.'

'No. This is fine.'

I felt another stab of alarm. 'Oh?'

The waitress came back. 'Are we too late to eat?'

Jean-Pierre asked. She looked at him; smiled. 'Oh, go on then. If you're quick.'

We looked at the menus. Jean-Pierre said: 'The lasagne for me. And orange juice.'

'I'll have the same.'

'D'you want garlic bread?'

The swing doors slapped again.

I longed to check my eczema. I said: 'So what's up?'

His eyes met mine. 'I wanted to apologise. About last week.'

'Well –' I smiled. I felt relieved. 'It wasn't ideal.' I shrugged. 'But how are you?'

'I'm okay.' I saw something odd in his eyes. A hardness – even dislike. 'We're okay.'

I stared at him.

He looked at me harder. 'Simone and I are okay.'

I gave a half-laugh. 'How do you mean?'

'Two orange juice,' sang the waitress. She came through the doors, releasing a snatch of laughter from the kitchen. 'Won't be a sec with your mains.' She went to the window and tried to force it open. A bluebottle fell from the casement. 'Bloody hell! Oops! Sorry!' Giggling, she swished into the kitchen.

Jean-Pierre cleared his throat. 'What I'm trying to say, Lottie, is that what went on was – none of your business.'

I frowned. 'But you've ended it with Patty?'

'What I'm saying, with respect, is that it's none of your business.'

I blinked. 'But you're cheating on Simone!'

He touched his tongue to his lip. 'Lottie,' he said. 'What I'm trying to say is that there are things that you don't understand. And this is one of them.' He flicked a glance at me. 'And I'd appreciate it if you didn't mention to anyone what I told you about my father.'

'I said I wouldn't!' I frowned. 'But that's – Jean-Pierre, I'm – you expect me to keep quiet about this? What do you want me to do when I go with her to Anton Lord's –'

Something in his face made me stop. He said: 'I think it might be for the best, actually, if you don't come.'

'Don't go?'

'Would you mind?'

I laughed in astonishment. 'Because I know about Patty?'

'Because –' He raised his hands.

I said: 'But have you ended it with Patty?'

He gave an irritated gesture.

'Do you have any idea how hurt Simone would be if she found out?'

'Please don't tell me how Simone would feel.'

'Have you ended it?'

He frowned.

'Have you ended it?'

'Just leave it, Lottie!'

'Have you ended it?'

'Here you go!' carolled the waitress. She slapped a brown plastic tray on the table and took off two plates of lasagne. 'Do you want ketchup?'

'No,' Jean-Pierre said.

There was silence. Beyond the windows thin devils, or perhaps angels, perched on the blackened stone columns. The wasps had stormed the lid of the wheelie bin. To the right a path disappeared into a dark wood.

'You know I'm going to have to tell her,' I said.

Jean-Pierre cut a piece of his lasagne. He closed his eyes for a second. 'Lottie. These things are not simple.'

'I will. I promise you.'

He looked at me with a kind of contempt. 'I don't doubt it.'

The waitress came back and rattled the window again. 'Oh!' she exclaimed. She went out.

'Things are not simple,' Jean-Pierre repeated. He looked away and his face was suddenly ineffably sad. 'Things are not always black and white.'

'I think they are.'

He looked back at me. His eyes were ashy now – seemed to have seen things that I would never see. 'I know you do,' he said. 'I sometimes think you have no idea how much damage your certainty can do.' He paused. 'I don't think you have any idea how much damage it has already done.'

'What's that supposed to mean?'

He paused again, and then I knew for sure that he disliked me – that he always had. Then he said softly: 'To your marriage. Your job. Your friendships. Why must you always push people away?'

'I will tell her,' I promised as the blush heated

227

my cheeks and my eyes pricked with tears. 'And Mark will be just gutted by what you've done.'

He put down his knife with an exasperated chink. 'Do you hate her so much? That you can't let anyone else be happy? What is it, Lottie? That she's prettier than you, and frankly nicer?'

It was too much. 'Fuck you!' I cried.

I ran into the corridor and out to the courtyard. The rain was streaming in cold white gusts and I fought through it to the car park. By the time I had started the engine it was so thick I could hardly breathe.

CHAPTER 19

That night I decided to have nothing more to do with the lot of them. Jean-Pierre was a shit; Patty Belle a manipulative bitch. So much for being sweet and guileless – she had clearly planned the thing from the start. I drank a bottle of Rioja while watching a documentary on lynchings in New Orleans, ate a bag of dried apricots, got diarrhoea and went to bed.

I woke with a sore throat that became a vicious cold. I spent three miserable days inside, and then, driven out by the empty fridge, bumped into Anton Lord getting take-away at Nando's. I had seen him only once since Patty's birthday dinner, dancing attendance on the editor of the *Daily Mail* in the lobby of Northcliffe House – then he had ignored me. Now, perhaps embarrassed to be caught waiting at a Portuguese restaurant, he stalked up to peck me on the cheek.

'I didn't know you lived near here.'

'Just round the corner.'

'Oh, yes.' He glanced over my shoulder. 'I've got the builders in.'

'I've got flu.'

'Oh.' He stepped back sharply. 'Have you heard about Patty?'

'No.'

'Oh, yes. You fell out, didn't you.' He glanced at the delivery counter and adjusted smeared rimless glasses. 'Well: she's gone bonkers. She cracked J-P's windscreen with a torch. Turned into a total bunny boiler. Mind you, I'm not surprised.'

'She cracked his windscreen with a *what*?'

'A torch. You know what a torch is?'

'But why?'

'Well, he ended it.' He turned round at the sound of his number being called and accepted a stained brown bag of chicken. 'Did the right thing. She's dangerous, that one.' A cross expression crumpled his small features. 'I must say he has a remarkable effect on women.'

'So where's she now?'

'With Mark David.' He rolled his eyes. 'What a loser. Don't know why he puts up with it.'

'Well, I suppose he doesn't know.'

'No.' He glanced at his watch. 'Anyway. You're coming to my launch, I hear.'

'If that's okay.'

'It should be. I'll send you an invite.'

He turned to peer into his stained brown bag of chicken. Then frowned at the window, illuminated by an other-worldly flashing. 'Oh, *fuck*!' I watched, with some satisfaction, as he ran out and tossed his tiny arms at the tow truck.

So he had dumped her. I chewed on the news

with my chicken. And she had smashed his wind-screen. And Mark didn't know. I couldn't help feeling sorry for her. Poor Patty. She had really loved him . . . But it was for the best. The question was if Simone had found out. Or Mark.

As the days went on I continued to wonder. But I had no one to ask. Jean-Pierre was out of the question. I thought of Tyrone but had no way to contact him. I didn't dare to ring Simone . . .

All that week I heard nothing. Then I saw a picture of Patty and Mark in the diary of the Saturday *Telegraph*. They were smiling at the camera – her radiantly, him rigidly, his arm stiffly behind her back. He was not standing close to her, but that didn't mean anything.

'Playwright Mark David with his model girl-friend at the launch of the new Gucci shop yesterday in Sloane Street,' read the caption. So. They were still together. I scrutinised the photo. She didn't look miserable. But it was impossible to tell.

Anton Lord's launch party was ten days later. It was December, and the place was decorated for Christmas. White fairy lights lay along the booths. Flashing stars hung over the long metal bar, where a raucous crowd stood shouting and knocking back champagne. A less jovial atmosphere characterised the space beyond, where clumps of nervous-looking men in glasses, IT people presumably, stood clutching flutes as if about to be interviewed.

Simone hadn't arrived and I was about to retreat to the loo when Queenie Holmes tapped me on the shoulder. 'Hi,' she said in her dreary voice. 'I thought it was you. How are you?'

'Not too bad. You?'

'Oh, you know. It's a very weird party. I don't know a soul.'

It looked pretty normal to me. Jowly men in suits greeted each other with enthusiastic hand-claps. Girls in tattered mini skirts and cowboy boots smoked looking bored. I had just spotted an acquaintance who wrote about European royalty and impoverished English aristocrats for *Tatler* when the crowd shifted and I saw Anton Lord. He was holding forth, the bristles on his bald head and the signet ring on his finger glinting in the light.

'There's Anton,' Queenie said. 'He's doing well, isn't he?'

'I suppose so.'

'But he was always going to.' Her eyes roamed the room. 'So how's Patty?'

'We fell out.'

She looked at me with more interest. 'Did you? Me too. She's a real bitch, isn't she? My boyfriend was like, "She's so sweet, she's had such a hard time." I was like, "Yeah, right. I'm never leaving *you* with her in the same room."'

'I know what you mean.'

'D'she go after your boyfriend?'

'No, I just – found out something.'

'About her and Jean-Pierre?'

'You knew?'

'Everyone knew. I thought she was seeing an adman.'

Jean-Pierre came up. He saw me and his expression changed. 'Hello.'

'Hi.'

'Oh, *hi*,' Queenie drawled. She kissed him with languid enthusiasm. 'We were just talking about Patty.'

Jean-Pierre glanced at the floor.

'I was saying she was a real bitch.'

Jean-Pierre moved his hand in a gesture of dismissal. His eyes, dampened by something – apology? regret? sorrow? – met mine. 'How are you?' he asked in a low voice.

'Okay.'

A deep red scratch ran down the back of his hand. Suddenly I felt sorry for him. I wondered how he got home. I said: 'Is Simone here?'

He nodded reluctantly and indicated behind me. Mark David was standing beside the bar with a champagne glass, his cheek smudged in shadow. Simone was beating the air passionately with her hand to make a point. She was in a big red sweater and boots.

'I'll see you later,' Queenie said. She drifted into the crowd.

I looked at Jean-Pierre. 'You did it, then.'

He nodded. 'Yes.'

'Well done.'

233

Without warning the music leapt in volume and the lights dimmed. A man in a striped jacket and torn jeans whooped and struggled onto the bar.

'There you are!' Simone cried. She had bags under her eyes and had cut her hair. It made her face look masculine and less attractive. But she seemed cheerful. She put her arm around me and gave a wry grimace. 'What a party. I feel about a hundred years old. I don't seem to know what to say to anyone.'

'I never do anyway.'

'But I said to Jean, "We have to go out! We're turning into hermits!"'

Jean-Pierre looked at her and she smiled at him. She turned back to me. 'Sorry to be late. I've been so wanting to see you.'

'And me you. I love your hair.'

'Oh, no! I look like a Cossack guard!'

'You look lovely,' Jean-Pierre said.

Simone touched my dress. 'Is this new?'

'From Voyage.'

'Oh, I want to go there. Will they let me in?'

'I'm sure. We can go together.'

'So is Anton going to make millions?'

'Probably.'

'He's very excited.'

She glanced at Jean-Pierre. 'Okay?'

'I want to go,' Jean-Pierre said.

'But we just got here!'

'But it's dreadful.'

I think he was afraid I would tell Simone there and then.

'He's in a very strange mood,' Simone said. She smiled at him. 'I can't do right for doing wrong.'

'You do everything right.'

She raised her eyebrows in surprise. Then smiled at me. 'See? All these compliments. Out of nowhere.'

'You deserve them.'

'Now you're doing it.'

The speakers crackled and burst into a techno version of Dancing Girl. The man on the bar slipped and righted himself with an almighty twist of his foot. Several champagne flutes toppled to the floor.

I moved out of the path of a dancing couple and caught Mark's eye. 'Hello,' he said.

'Hi!'

'How are you?'

'Very well. Very well!'

I looked at him, but he seemed normal; and he went up to Jean-Pierre and Simone as if it was the most ordinary thing in the world. He put a pleased hand on Jean-Pierre's arm. 'How are you?'

Jean-Pierre's eyes gave a flash of alarm. 'Not too bad.'

'I hear you got that column.'

'That's right.'

'Congratulations.' He turned to Simone, his face tender. 'How nice to see you. You're looking well.'

Through the plate glass windows I saw a girl emerge from between two buses and stop under a lamp post outside the plate glass windows. She got something out of her bag, peered at it and outlined her mouth. A man went past her, turned his head and said something; she shook her head.

'You seem preoccupied,' Simone said.

I smiled at her. 'It's the music. I can't hear.'

'We're getting old. We should get up and dance.'

'I can't dance to this.'

'We should be taking ecstasy. Shouldn't we, Jean?'

'Shouldn't we what?'

'Take ecstasy.'

'Hello,' Patty breathed. Her dress glowed like snow. Her eyes locked on Jean-Pierre.

'Patty!' Simone cried. 'How are you?'

'I'm okay.'

She looked at Mark. He put a hand to her hair. 'Did you get the taxi all right?'

'Yes.'

She was simmering with that same excitement she had had in the pub, but now it had an almost fearsome edge. Her mouth was slightly open and her breath came fast. She did not acknowledge me. She was looking at Jean-Pierre. It was painful to watch – as if no one else existed.

Under the intensity of her gaze Jean-Pierre's face paled and his eyes dropped. But Mark just smiled at her genially. 'Well. We need to get you some fizz. Can we get anyone else a glass?'

236

He and Patty moved into the crowd. I gave an involuntary shiver. Jean-Pierre knocked back his champagne. He was looking at no one in particular.

'I hear you fell out,' Simone said softly.

I went cold. 'Yes.'

'I'm sorry to hear that.'

'It was one of those things.'

'She's moved out?'

I nodded.

'That's a shame. She's so alone.'

'I want to go,' Jean-Pierre interrupted. It was now a command, not a statement, and Simone looked at him in surprise.

She smiled tolerantly. 'Okay. But I was just saying to Lottie – she's very guileless, Patty. She's like a child.'

Jean-Pierre snorted. 'Oh, yes.'

'I feel sorry for her.'

'Can we go now?'

'Okay! But let's just wait for Mark.'

He looked at her intently. 'I love you. Will you remember that?'

She looked at him with pleased perplexity. 'Of course!' She raised her eyebrows at me. 'Can I at least go to the loo?'

And so we were alone.

'Don't worry,' I said. 'I'm not going to tell her!'

'Excuse me!' barked a waitress. And it was as we stepped out of her way that Patty took her chance. She rushed up to Jean-Pierre and took him by the arms. She said something to him – I couldn't hear what, but it was clearly an appeal. Every fibre of her body strained with the intensity of it – as I watched her thin shoulder strap popped from the seam. She didn't notice; it was, I reflected bitterly, the first time she had not deliberately been sexual.

I looked at Mark David. He had his back to us at the bar.

Jean-Pierre jerked free. Patty's expression changed; she held out her hands; leaned forward. 'No!' his lips commanded – and Mark came up.

He looked from one to the other in mild surprise. 'I've given up,' he said. 'It's perfectly impossible to get served.' He looked at Patty. 'Are you all right, my dear?'

She nodded, not looking at him. She seemed on the verge of tears.

'You don't look it.' He put his white hand to her forehead. 'Do you want some water?'

'No!' She shook him off.

Before Mark could react Anton Lord appeared. 'Come to the Atlantic!' he ordered. His shirt was stretched tight over his paunch and buttoned up wrong; his lips glistened with alcohol.

'What's the Atlantic?' Mark asked.

'A bar,' I said. 'On Piccadilly.' I looked at Jean-Pierre. He had his hands in his pockets; his face was a mask of misery.

'I've not heard of it.'

'Of what?' Simone asked, coming up. She yawned. 'That loo is very weird.'

'The Atlantic,' Mark said. 'Anton wants us to go.'

'Then let's!'

Jean-Pierre froze. 'No. We're going home.'

'We can go for a bit, can't we?'

'Yes,' Patty said.

I stared at her with hatred.

'Let's go home,' I said.

'It'll be fun,' Simone urged. 'You said you wanted to go out.'

'Why not?' Mark David agreed expansively. Circles of red stood like crayon on his cheeks. Was he drunk, or on edge? Surely he hadn't guessed? The situation had the inherent tension of crystal glass.

Jean-Pierre's jaw twitched. It was impossible for him to say no; and so we left in a ragged group. It was then that my throat began to tickle feverishly, as if a piece of toothpick was caught in it; and as we stood hailing cabs in the street I coughed the same dry irritable cough over and over.

'You take that one,' Anton ordered as a taxi came up, 'and we'll follow.'

I was with Patty and Mark. As we clattered past the brightly decorated Christmas windows I continued to give that dry tormenting cough. Patty didn't look at me; her gaze was fixed on the black glass or, when forced by necessity, on Mark. What the hell did she have in mind? As if to emphasise my sense of impending jeopardy, it had begun to pour with rain. The drops bounced like pennies on the windscreen and drilled on an accident by the park – an ambulance had smashed into a red Peugeot 205. The driver, a Muslim woman, huddled in her headdress in the torch-lit lee of the door.

'Fancy an ambulance causing an accident,' I said, and for a second Patty's eyes met mine. Her face was ashen. Then she turned back to the cold window, pressing her lips together.

In Regent Street we inched under an illuminated tree, three flashing wise men, a white line of stars. Not once did Patty blink. She seemed almost possessed. I had no idea what was on her mind. Did she want to force a showdown with Jean-Pierre? To steal him from Simone? Had she lost all self-control? I had no idea. It occurred to me that I had never known her at all . . .

At the Atlantic Simone put her head, wet and elated, through the window of the taxi. 'They won't let us in. We're going to Momo.'

'Where's Momo?'

'Heddon Street. See you there.'

It was a restaurant got up like a souk in a courtyard. The basement was divided into booths by red velvet curtains. Smooth young faces looked up enquiringly through a brown haze of smoke.

'This is fun!' Simone cried. She sat cross-legged

240

on the cushions, smiling at Jean-Pierre. 'Okay, *chéri?*'

Jean-Pierre met Patty's gaze. I think if he could have thrust a dagger into her side at that minute he would have. 'Fine,' he said.

Mark picked up the dirty little menu and passed it to Patty. 'What would you like, dear?'

Patty sank down her eyes. A beading of sweat frosted her lip. 'A Mojito.'

'Two Mojitos,' Mark ordered. 'Lottie? A Cosmopolitan? And two glasses of champagne?'

Jean-Pierre glanced at Patty. She stared back at him. I began to cough clearing my throat desperately. Simone looked at me in concern. 'You should take sage for that.'

'I'll be fine in a minute.'

'Do you want some water?'

With a jaunty rattle our drinks arrived. Mark smiled at Patty. 'What shall we drink to?'

She fingered her glass with taut fingers. 'To love.'

'Love?' Simone exclaimed. 'That's nice.' She smiled ruefully at Jean-Pierre. Then her eyes went to Patty and her expression changed.

'It's nice to see you both,' Mark was saying warmly. 'I've been worried about you. I felt too far away, stuck in New York. But you both look so well.'

Simone was looking at Jean-Pierre as if she had never seen him in her life.

'I get that feeling in New York,' I said. I cleared my throat. 'I feel dirty when I've been in

Manhattan too long. I get a kind of craving for grass.'

Simone put down her glass. 'I'm feeling very peculiar.'

I put my hand on her arm. 'What, ill?'

'We came past a terrible accident,' Mark remembered. 'An ambulance crashed into a Peugeot. The woman was lucky to survive.'

'A woman,' Jean-Pierre said. He lifted his buzzing glass coldly at Patty. 'Have you had enough over there?'

Her eyes met his with accusing hurt. 'No.'

She lit a cigarette and then looked at it and crushed it out.

'I can't believe it's a new millennium,' I said desperately. 'Has everyone made their plans? It's going to be so weird on New Year's Eve.'

'With all it holds,' Mark murmured.

In the silence we heard the rain rattling the windows.

'What a night,' Simone exclaimed. She twisted her hands wretchedly. 'Why am I so cold?'

Patty put down her glass. 'I need the toilet.'

'So do I,' Jean-Pierre said.

Her eyes fluttered like birds as he helped her to her feet. 'After you.'

As the curtains swung behind them I was tempted to call for help. The sense of danger was so strong I was amazed Mark hadn't rung the police.

But he seemed quite oblivious. I was reminded

of my own denial about the copywriter. Were we all so blind? I looked at Simone. At once. I knew that she wasn't – that she had seen it all. 'I'm amazed there aren't more accidents,' Mark was saying amiably. A tuft of his hair was standing on end, lending him comic-book innocence, like Tintin, or Charlie Brown. 'Ambulance-drivers drive like maniacs these days. I saw a police car hit a lorry last year. Was I with you?'

He looked at Simone. She came to attention with an effort. 'Eh?'

'When the police car hit that Tesco lorry in Oxford. Was I with you?'

Simone put a hand on his knee – seemed about to answer. Then she got to her feet. The curtains swung sharply behind her.

Mark stared after her in surprise. Then he blinked and frowned. 'Tired, I expect,' he said. He adjusted his glasses. 'How is the novel?'

'Still going.'

He nodded, absently lining up the menu. 'Yes? I wanted to – um –' He put his hand in his jacket pocket. 'It seems an opportune moment to talk about Patty.'

I went cold. 'How do you mean?'

'Well, she's rather . . . down. About, um.' He thrummed his fingers on the table. 'Your . . . dispute.'

'Oh!' I gave a wry snort. 'Is she.'

He nodded. 'Now, I don't want to know what it was about, as I've told her. And I've no wish to assign blame to either side. But it does seem a shame that –'

From the courtyard came a faint splintering of glass.

'You're not friends,' Mark David said.

I looked at him in disbelief. The evening was acquiring the absurdity of a farce. If it hadn't been so horrifying I might have laughed.

'Look,' I said. And began to cough. I took a gulp of Simone's glass. But still I couldn't stop. I could feel myself sweating. What was going on up there? Patty wasn't . . . ? I got to my feet.

'I'm going to the loo,' I said.

I carried the mental image of his surprised face down the dark corridor to the loos. But the Ladies' was coldly bare, white loo paper strewn on cracked brown tiles. I went up the stairs, into the convivial clamour of the restaurant. 'You waiting?' asked a waiter. 'No, no,' I said.

I went into the courtyard.

They were lit by a yellow streetlamp. Patty was on a bench shivering and looking frightened. Jean-Pierre was standing stiffly with his hands in his pockets. Simone had her back to a shop window glittering with fairy lights. Between them, on the ground, lay a red umbrella. It was bent at an unnatural angle. There was something disturbing about it, like a cat I had once seen with a broken neck.

'What's happening?' I asked.

Jean-Pierre shook his head. Patty looked at him. It was that look I can't forget. Illuminated by the dim light of the streetlamp it held a vast longing. Her face was sheer as a cliff. You could no more take your eyes off it than look at the darkness around the sun.

Simone gave a ragged sniff. 'You knew,' she said. My throat ached. 'Oh, Simone.'

She bent her head miserably, her eyes glistening.

'Sim!' Jean-Pierre pleaded. He put out his hand. 'Don't do this to yourself,' he begged. 'I love *you*.'

'He loves me too,' Patty said in a shaking voice.

Jean-Pierre shot her a glance of pure hatred. He stepped forward and grabbed Simone by the wrists. 'I love *you*,' he insisted passionately. He stared into her eyes as if there was print at the back of them. 'Do you understand?'

'He loves *me*,' Patty contradicted in a high voice. She stood up. 'He said so. While we were doing it.'

'Doing what?' Mark asked from behind me.

He glanced round, smiling uncertainly, and stepped forward.

Patty sat down abruptly. She held her bag on her lap. She seemed unsure what to do. 'Doing what?' Mark asked again.

'Sleeping with me,' Jean-Pierre said.

His sentence had the effect of a clap of thunder. In the silence that followed I felt a kind of relief – as if the tension had finally drained from the air. But Mark didn't seem to understand. He had his head on one side as if, underwater, he had heard a sound high on the surface.

'I didn't mean to!' Patty burst out. She clutched her bag desperately. 'It just happened! We couldn't help it!'

Mark frowned. He turned his head. 'When?'

'Since October,' Jean-Pierre said.

'Oh!' Simone exclaimed. It was the grunt of someone punched in the stomach.

What I couldn't understand was why Mark David wasn't more angry. The expression on his face could only be described as pitying. 'Is it his?' he asked.

Patty put her hands over her face.

'Is what his?' Simone asked. 'Is *what* his?'

'Patty's pregnant,' Mark David told her in a soft voice. He looked at Patty with a different expression. 'Is it his?'

'Are you having Jean's *baby*?' Simone cried. She put her hand to her mouth. 'Are you having Jean's *baby*?'

'Yes,' Patty said. She stepped backward, her hands on her stomach, her eyes triumphant.

They faltered, though, at Simone. It was as if she had realised the enormity of what she'd done. 'Oh, Mark,' she sobbed. 'I'm so unhappy!'

From the street I heard the faint hopeful sound of carol singing.

I felt weirdly transported. I said to Jean-Pierre: 'But what about your father?'

They all looked at me. I said: 'Didn't you think about that?'

Jean-Pierre stared at me with loathing. Simone threw her head back. 'What *about* his father?'

Something drove me on. 'His mental illness,' I said.

Patty froze. 'What mental illness?'

Jean-Pierre clenched his jaw. He said in a low voice: 'My father was psychotic.'

'Oh my God!' Patty cried. She began hiccuping. 'Oh my God!'

Simone just looked at Jean-Pierre.

Patty got to her feet. She plucked at Mark David's sleeve. 'I want to go home,' she begged. 'Please take me home!'

Mark David looked at Simone and then Jean-Pierre. He seemed to be considering his decision.

'Oh, for God's sake!' I burst out.

Mark turned to look at me. His expression was hidden by the shadow of the lamp post. 'I knew this would happen,' he said.

Patty gave a despairing sob. Sniffling, she rattled his arm. 'I didn't mean to!'

'But you did,' I scolded Patty. 'And that's what you always do! Hurt people and feel sorry later!'

'That's enough!' Mark snapped. 'I'm sorry,' he said, and I realised after a second he was talking to Simone. He touched her cheek with infinite kindness. Then, as if shouldering a burden, he took Patty's arm. 'Come, then,' he said. Hiccuping faintly, she shuffled beside him toward the alley. The night was cool now; above us the moon hung in a pockmarked circle. On the far side of the courtyard the dark bushes massed under a blue night sky. It smelled of wet gunmetal.

As their footsteps receded I realised I shouldn't be there. I went up to Simone. 'I'll – leave you now.'

She only nodded. I went the other way out of the courtyard, stiffly, without looking back. Sitting on the torn seat of the taxi I had the sense that my youth was over for good. And so we clattered towards the dawn.

That I got a taxi straightaway was the reason, I realised later, that I reached my house ahead of Mark and Patty. I was just in front of them – had just paid off my cab when their taxi, an old brown one, rattled round the corner. It was two am, chilly and still.

I learned later why they had followed me. Mark had driven Patty to my house at the start of the evening, apparently, to get his spare key, which she had left on the rack in my utility room. But I was out. So they left his car there and took a cab.

But I didn't know that as the taxi pulled up yards from where I was standing. Two dim figures moved in the back and then the door opened. Patty! I thought, and I had the ridiculous idea that she had come to see me, that time could be rewound and everything put back.

Then Mark followed her onto the pavement. His

breath hung in the air as he counted out the fare with faint chinks. The taxi drove away and they looked at each other, a look of understanding; not together, but not apart either – in some kind of accord.

He seemed about to speak when I saw the other man. The moon picked out the bulk of his shoulders and the grey of his hair. Patty gave a gasp. Mark looked alarmed. He stepped forward.

'Now, look here!' he exclaimed.

Kaplan knocked him aside like a ninepin. He seemed consumed by anger – burned up with it. He growled at Patty: 'Didn't I tell you not to talk?'

She began shaking. She backed away, making small terrified noises in her throat. Once she stumbled and, on a high note of terror, righted herself and ran on.

Kaplan caught her at the end of the road. But she pulled free with a scream. They disappeared round the corner.

The tramp pulling the broken wheelie suitcase got to her first. He was rolling her over with shaking hands, his red scarf brushing her throat.

Her hair strewed the hard kerb and a gout of blood welled from her cheek.

'The fucking cunt! The fucking, fucking cunt,' the tramp swore in anger and disbelief and I could hear his hoarse sobbing breath as he lifted her head and cradled it in his hands. 'Call an ambulance!' he barked. 'Call an ambulance!'

On the corner I ran into Mark David.

'He got her,' I said urgently. 'We need an ambulance!'

'Where is she?'

'There! Do you have a phone?'

He ran limping towards her and knelt on the pavement. When he got out his phone I saw that his forehead was bleeding and that he had a scraped, bloody ear. 'Yes,' he said into it. 'Ambulance, please.' He stroked Patty's hair back from her forehead and then glanced up at me. 'Where did he go?'

'I don't know.'

He raised his head. 'He must be here somewhere.'

But the street was still, the car roofs strung like pale pearls in the moonlight. High up above a yellow window snapped black. In the distance I heard a tentative warble: the first bird of dawn.

The siren broke the silence. It grew and grew until the lights swung into our eyes and two men in yellow jackets were telling us to step back. 'Who's going with her?' one asked.

I had raised my hand at Mark and saw he was shaking his head.

I felt a stab of apprehension and something else – amazement, surprise. 'You're not going?'

His face was wretched. 'I can't.'

'Well, we can't wait,' said the man briskly.

'Then I'll go!' I cried.

As the ambulance pulled away I had a last glimpse of Mark. He was standing in an odd way, his hands clasped as if he was praying, and then he dropped his head abruptly. As the ambulance turned the corner he began limping clumsily away. So I left him in the moonlight – pacing the paths of his own Gethsemane.

CHAPTER 20

'Will you give this to Mark?' Patty greeted me.

I was by a grimy double glazed window. It framed a litter-strewn alley and an open fire door where a man was leaning, smoking a cigarette pinched between his thumb and his forefinger. Inside, green, red and yellow paper chains looped the wall in uneven semicircles. A white plastic Christmas tree leant in the corner. Even in the hospital it was Christmas.

'Of course I will,' I said.

I took the letter and tears pricked my throat. Her hair was thin at her temples and I saw that her beauty was fading. Beneath the yellow bruises the fine lines were apparent around her eyes and the skin sagged slightly on her jaw. A pad between her legs stemmed the bleeding. But she seemed cheerful – hopeful even, in that unforgiving fluorescent glare.

'I'm sorry,' she said. 'About everything.' She looked at me with bright eyes. 'I lost the baby.'

I nodded, tears coming to my own eyes. 'I know.'

She nodded, swallowing. 'Well. Maybe it was for

the best. I don't know if I'd have been a very good mummy.' She blinked and wiped her eyes. She looked fixedly at the bed in an effort of control.

'You'd have been a great mum,' I said in a high voice, and I couldn't hold back the tears.

She pressed her lips together. 'I wanted to be.' Her face crumpled. 'I would have loved it. But. I guess it wasn't meant to be. Do you have a tissue?'

She blew her nose. 'I don't know,' she said, and her face crumpled again. She swallowed hard. 'I'm having such funny dreams. Last night I dreamed I had a fatal illness and my mum was giving me some tablets and I knew if I took them I'd die. I said: "Aren't I even allowed to deteriorate?"' Her eyes overflowed and tears trickled down her cheeks. She said: 'Have you seen Mark?'

'Mark?' I sniffed. 'He's not very well.'

'He's left me, hasn't he?'

'Of *course* not!'

She just looked at me. It was terrible to remember that look. It was clear that she knew the truth and that she accepted it as her fate, and that, more than anything else, was what made it so awful. She licked her cracked lips and something imperceptible in her seemed to harden, as if she were summoning up all her old acting skills, all her resolve. 'But, gosh,' she said. 'I'm glad I'm here. Everyone's so friendly. And the food is really nice, all my favourites, and the nurses are so kind.' She let out a sob. 'I'm very lucky.'

I took her hand and held it. 'Oh my dear.'

She swallowed and looked at me painfully. 'But I can't seem to stop thinking. I lie here in the dark and I remember and sometimes it's so awful.' Her eyes darkened. 'Have you ever done something you can't seem to forget?' Her breath came ragged. 'I'm so ashamed.'

'Now,' I said strongly. 'You mustn't be. You're wonderful. You just have to concentrate on getting better.'

'But Mark's left me,' she said, and I was struck silent – we met at a deeper truth, an assent, unspoken. She tried to smile. 'It's funny, isn't it, life. I read a book about suicide once called *The Myth of* – something. Which said death was the only philosophical problem. But I don't think that's true. Living is just as much of one.' She moved her head on the pillow: her neck seemed to be hurting. 'Once I had a suicide pact with a man called Lemar. And you know what he did? He jumped without calling me!'

'Time for your medicine,' said the nurse, wheeling up a trolley.

'Do you need me to go?'

'It's probably best. We'll do the bath in a minute.'

'But I want her to stay!'

'She can come back tomorrow.'

'You will come?' Patty cried. I heard her behind me, voice rising. 'You will come?'

I was at the end of the corridor when I burst into tears. I seemed to be crying everywhere those days – getting dressed, making the tea, writing my book. It felt like I couldn't stop. I ran into the toilets, and leaned against the wall. A black hair lay across the sink. The Asian doctor with the scuffed shoes and sad tortoise eyes had caught me leaving the Ladies' after a similar crying fit the day before. 'Doesn't she have any family?' he had asked, and I saw in his eyes the incomprehension – what kind of world did she live in? 'She needs visitors! She's very low!'

But there was no one. I had been round to Joyce's. But there was no answer, and a neighbour, a neat blonde, maybe Swedish, said she'd gone to India three months before. I only had an old mobile number for Tyrone, though I was going through the phone book – I knew he worked in a salon in Maida Vale. And Mark David had gone back to Christine.

I had come back from the hospital that first morning to find him on the doorstep.

His face was pale. 'How is she?'

I gave a sob. 'How do you think she is? She's – fucked up!'

He put his hands wearily to his face.

I stared at him. 'Are you going to see her?'

He shook his head. 'It wouldn't be right.'

'But you don't have to be together! I know she was wrong! But she needs people!'

'I don't know *what* to do!' he burst out.

'*See* her! I thought you loved her.'

'I do love her.'

'Then go.'

'I can't!' he burst out, and I remembered what I had forgotten – that he was Catholic. 'I have prayed about it,' he said, and I could see the pain in his face. 'Don't think I haven't prayed. Don't think I can't bear it.' He put down a bag. 'Please pass these on,' he said formally. 'Forgive me, but I think you have my spare key.'

It had begun to snow when I came back out on the path. The flakes caught in his hair. 'I won't ever forget her,' he said in a low voice, as if he were making a pledge. Then, to himself: 'I could never make her happy.'

That afternoon I had my first stroke of luck. On my sixth salon, an establishment called The Kutting Klub and Beauty Plaice, a hoarse female voice conceded they used to have someone called Tyrone.

'Kyle,' she roared over the whirr of dryers, 'D'you have that number for Ty?'

She came back on the line. 'She 'asn't got it. But Kyle says you can get him at a salon called Angie's on the Shepherd's Bush Road.'

There was no Angie's in the book, but there was an Andee's. They took a message and said he would be in the following day. I ate Alpen that night in front of the TV, and passed out before the news.

When I reached Patty's bed the next day I saw she was in a bad way. Her face was yellow and her hands were ice-cold.

'It hurts,' she wept. 'It really hurts!'

The nurse was holding her hand. 'We're getting you some painkillers.'

'But it hurts!' Her eyes were full of beseeching astonishment.

'Perhaps tomorrow she'll be better,' the nurse told me kindly, and I took myself sorrowfully away.

But that afternoon she seemed better. Her face was still hollow but her eyes seemed calmer.

'I've been thinking,' she said. 'Ed could have killed Mark – couldn't he? On the pavement. Is that why he isn't talking to me?'

I felt my throat begin to ache. 'No.'

'Are you sure?' She looked at me fearfully. 'Because Ed getting in trouble was my fault too, wasn't it? I was so frightened. But I shouldn't have gone to the police.'

'Don't be ridiculous,' I said. I had no idea what she was talking about. 'Of course you should have.' Then I realised she didn't know what he had done – about the prostitute. 'He's not a nice man.'

'But I'm a bad girl! Because I betrayed Mark! And now he won't see me!' She gave a hectic sob. 'And all I want is to see him!'

'He will see you! Of course he will! You just need to get better.'

But she began tossing in the bed. 'Oh, God,' she wept. 'I'm bad, aren't I? I'm bad, I'm bad, I'm bad!'

'Dear, oh dear,' said the nurse. She took hold of her shoulders. 'What's all this? We'll do our examination in a minute.'

Patty clutched the sheet. 'Not inside?'

'I'm afraid so. It shouldn't be too uncomfortable, with the painkillers.'

She started weeping. 'I can't!'

'I'm afraid we have to,' the nurse told her. 'Just be a little bit brave. It's only a quick, sharp pain.'

'Tell him I'm sorry,' Patty pleaded, as I turned away. 'Tell him I'm really, really sorry!'

I couldn't think of anything else, as I wearily mopped up a flood in my kitchen. My washing machine had chosen that week of all weeks to pack up. As I went to call the plumber my phone rang. It was Tyrone.

He sounded less camp than I remembered. 'I heard you rang,' he said. 'How's tricks?'

'It's Patty. She's ill.'

'Ill?' His voice dimmed. 'Sorry,' he said, louder. 'What's she got?'

'She's in hospital.'

'In hospital? Why?'

'She's been hit.'

'Been what?'

'She's been hit. By Ed Kaplan.'

'Oh Jesus.'

'Yes,' I said. 'And he practically killed her.' I sniffed. 'Will you go and see her?'

'Well, of course.'

'Tomorrow?'

There was a second's pause. 'I'm off to Ibiza tomorrow. I could go tonight?'

'No, visiting hours are over today. But she'll be there tomorrow. From ten.'

'Ten?' The phone buzzed. He said in a cooler voice: 'Okay. Though I'm a teensy bit hacked off with her. She wasn't very nice last time I saw her. In fact she was an absolute bitch.'

The next day was bright. Brown branches stood against a clear sky. In the chill car the radio announced a thirty per cent chance of a white Christmas.

Patty looked like a stray cat. Her skin was dry and pouchy and her hands swollen like inflated washing-up gloves.

'I did a really bad thing,' she said. 'Will you say I'm sorry?'

I bent to catch the words. 'Who to?'

'Simone.' She moved her hand.

'Oh, sweetheart.'

'I know,' she said. 'I heard the nurses talk. They talk a lot – at night. About their boyfriends.' She smiled faintly. 'It's sweet, really. They're so . . . hopeful.'

'Now, look,' I said, 'this is silly.'

She wouldn't let me finish. 'Did you ever think you were dying?'

'Once.'

'When?'

'When my father crashed the Ferrari.'

'Were you frightened?'

I nodded.

She pondered. 'See, I don't mind dying. I always thought if I did I wouldn't feel anything any more – and it was always the feelings that hurt.' She moved her head on the pillow. 'Now I think maybe they were what it was all about. You know, maybe they were the happiness and I didn't see it. That the happiness was always there, like a scrap of feeling under all the other feelings. Because now I see that I *was* happy – in New York. That day you came and Mark and I made . . .' She clenched her hand in fury. '*What* were they called?'

'Rossinis,' I said in a cracked voice.

'Yes! Or that day in the pub with Jean-Pierre. I mean, okay, we fought; we always fought. But now I realise, we were happy, because we were alive, and together: we had this electric connection. Or when I took Simone to Hennes. Or me and Tyrone when he was sick.' She sighed, but this time it was the faint, ragged sigh of relief. 'It's funny, how you realise things too late. Someone once said to me the tragedy about life is that you understand it backwards. But I don't think so. I think the tragedy is there is no tragedy – you just don't know it till you die.'

'Oh, honey,' I said. I thought she was talking nonsense.

'I always felt like I was waiting for something,' she went on. 'What do you think it was?'

'Love?'

She nodded. 'Love. And now I know I had it.'

I was about to ask if she meant Mark or Jean-Pierre when her face changed and I saw Tyrone. He had got himself a gold front tooth: it gleamed bizarrely in his mouth and made him look more like a child-freak than ever: his forehead bulged and a love bite decorated his neck.

But Patty lit up at the sight of him. She turned her head slowly, her eyes bright.

'Hey sweetheart.' He sat on the bed. 'Look at *you*. Don't *you* look pretty.'

'Those for me?'

'You bet. So, honey bunch. I hear you've been scrapping.'

She raised her tight hands for his flowers. 'Everything kind of came back on me.'

'You doofus.'

'*You* said I should tell them! D'you want some juice?'

'Ooh, yes please.' He settled himself more comfortably. 'I tell you, there's an über-bitch in that the flower shop downstairs. I batted my eyes in the most winsome way and she *ripped* away my credit card. And she's not even old. It's unbeliev-able someone could become so twisted in such a short time. But the good news is that my parents are coming to stay. The only problem is the flat is a disaster. The guest bathroom is heaving with hair. And the *kitchen. Acid* will not shift the stains.'

I stood. 'I'll leave you to it.'

I bent to kiss Patty's bruised forehead. Which I was glad I did, because the next day, when I came in, they said she was gone.

CHAPTER 21

The small Scottish sister with the pale eyelashes was the one who told me. But I checked the story with both nurses. They confirmed he was middle-aged, grey-haired, with – according to the Scottish sister – 'bonny blue eyes'.

She had left of her own accord. 'We told them it was a hazard,' she assured me, nodding earnestly, her chapped hand on my arm. 'But they wouldnae listen. He talked to her for maybe an hour or more, and she'd got a bit of colour in her cheeks, like she'd a bit of hope in her again.'

'Did she leave a note?'

'No. But they left real quick. It was right after the ward round, he said he'd a car outside; and he seemed like a gorgeous guy. He was hangin' onto her like he was madly in love. We all agreed she'd a good one there. And we cannae stop them if they want to be gone, even if they shouldnae be out of bed; we may look it, but we're no' a jail.'

She looked at me sympathetically. 'She didnae warn you.'

'No.'

'Well, she'll no doubt call. And you mustnae fret; she was on the mend. In a day or two we'd ha' let her go anyway.'

'But you're sure she wasn't – kidnapped?'

She burst out laughing, and then clapped her hand on her mouth at my expression. 'I don't think so, sweetheart. You shoulda seen 'em together. Her eyes were like wee candles.'

But she never did call. It was a strange ending – weird, unsatisfying, nothing explained or made right.

Except that I felt that I had . . . made things right. Those last days with Patty had taught me a lesson, one of life's intangible lessons that are so hard to put into words. They had taught me the power of love; the healing of forgiveness; the need to keep on going when the worst has happened. From that soil, it wouldn't be too exaggerated to say, I finally found the root of love.

The irony was that it was later that winter I realised that she had slept with my boyfriend. I mean the copywriter. Funny how these things come to you. I just understood it, suddenly, when I woke up in the middle of the night. I didn't even mind. Not really.

I spent that Christmas at my mother's, with her boyfriend, a yachting man who wore cravats and talked about golf. The day after Boxing Day I came home. I was reading Erich Fromm's *The Art of Loving* when my doorbell rang. On the wet path, clutching a red bowling bag, stood a girl with bleached hair and a big nose. She looked at me challengingly. 'Do you know who I am?'

'No,' I said. I didn't.

'I'm Melania.' Her mittened hand suddenly tightened on the strap and I was reminded of Patty's hand clenching as she fought to remember – what was it? – the cocktail she had made in New York. Typical Patty! I thought.

'Hi,' I said. Then realised. It was Ed Kaplan's daughter.

'I'm looking for Patty,' she said, and her face constricted suddenly in an effort to appear cool. She was, I realised, only about sixteen, though she had the full bust, the big hair, the pancake foundation of a woman in her forties. 'I got the address from Joseph,' she said. 'My dad's advisor. Is she here?'

I had no idea what to say.

'She is here, right?' she demanded, and this time she couldn't hide her fear. Her eyes stared at me, scared between thick black lashes. 'I know she's here,' she said. 'Don't say she's not. I won't tell Mom.'

'She's not, I'm afraid.'

She stepped forward. 'But this is where she lives, right? You don't need to pretend; I know. I know everything. I really like Patty. She's been great to me. Much nicer than *Mom*. She bought me a thong. She introduced me to Miss Collier.'

I cleared my throat. 'Miss Collier?'

'Her acting coach. I'm going to be an actress. Like her.'

'Oh, right.'

'Miss *Collier* says she's like an enchanted child. Miss *Collier* says she has a lovely talent wandering through her like a jailed spirit.' She rubbed her nose. 'I'm going to be like her, now I've got away from *Mom*.'

'The thing is,' I said – how to let this overgrown child down gently? – 'she's really not here. She moved out. I'm afraid I don't know where she is.'

She frowned. 'You don't?'

'I really don't.'

'Oh, my,' she said and her breath clouded the air. She rubbed her arm, goose-bumped in the cold. 'I don't have anywhere else to go,' she said. 'I don't have anywhere else to try.'

The copywriter was late, as always. He threw his blue Porsche up onto the pavement and strode through the arch. His hair was longer; he was in a suit I'd never seen. He wheeled to a halt. 'Hello, stranger.'

'If I ask you one question,' I said, 'will you give me the honest answer?'

'Yes,' he said.

'Did you sleep with Patty?'

He hesitated for an instant, and I knew that he had. 'No,' he said.

'I don't believe you.'

'Dear, dear.' He draped an arm round my shoulders. 'My dear Charlotte. Surely you haven't been winding yourself up over that?'

We were in the cloisters of St Mary Abbot's on Kensington High Street – it was Millennium Eve. He looked admiringly at the ruby stained-glass windows. 'So she went back to Kaplan,' he said. 'Poor fool.'

'How did you know?'

He indicated an angel, head bowed sorrowfully to her chest. 'Charming . . . Anton told me. It was inevitable, I suppose. She was like a moth to a flame.'

'I don't know,' I said. 'I think he might have forced her. I think he might have –' I didn't want to voice my worst thoughts.

But he shook his head. 'She always carried a torch for him,' he said. 'God knows why. She once asked me how she'd be remembered. I said, as an enchanting child.' Experimentally, he blew out a white plume of air. 'You know she was Meena Saragoussi?'

'Meena Saragoussi?'

'Do you know who I mean?'

I stared at a pigeon pecking a slab of stone. I did know who he meant. I supposed it was possible – almost certainly true. Some of the comments that Kaplan made came back to me. '*Then just understand this. You cannot talk.*' And Patty: '*I was so frightened. But I shouldn't have gone to the police.*'

'My God,' I said. 'Then he probably has killed her.'

The copywriter shook his head. 'No, he loved

her. He did actually love her. He was a con-man, like her father.'

'How do you know?' I asked.

'She told me.'

'When?'

'We used to talk. I felt rather sorry for her.'

'Is that right,' I said.

The pigeon waddled towards us. It had a pink nub where its left foot should have been. It was sharp-eyed and tousled with dirt.

'I think I might get married,' the copywriter said. 'Next year. I haven't asked her yet.'

I gave a bitter snort. 'But you think she'll say yes?'

'Oh, it's not Tiffany. Pippa's an artist. She's young. Twenty-five. You'd like her.'

'I somehow doubt that.'

'Well, perhaps not.'

He strode to the gate.

Jean-Pierre rang the day after New Year. 'I just spoke to Mark,' he said. 'What a mess.'

'That's one word for it.'

'I had no idea.'

'No.'

'Is she all right now?'

'She's with Ed Kaplan.'

'I beg your pardon?'

'She went back to Ed Kaplan. She lost the child.'

We met at Jac's Bar on Lonsdale Road. It was a trendy place, got up like a library, with fish flickering in mossy tanks. The barman was a light-eyed man with a lilting, Welsh-valley voice and an acne-rough neck. When he saw us he put down a copy of *Mastering Futures Trading*. 'You know it's a bubble,' he told Jean-Pierre.

'What is?'

'The Internet boom. It's like tulips in the seventeenth century. You should sell your shares.'

'I don't have any.'

We took armchairs by the wall.

The news had finally pierced Jean-Pierre's gold-plated self-possession: he stumbled on his words. 'Why didn't you tell me?' he demanded.

'Why didn't you ask?'

'You could have rung!' He put up his hands in apology. 'Sorry. I know. It was all so crazy. We just jumped on a plane. I knew it was my only chance to save our marriage.' He flicked up his eyes. 'So what happened?'

I told him.

He said: 'That's terrible,' and the 'terrible' began as a growl and went high. He cleared his throat. 'Thank God she didn't have the baby.'

'Why on earth do you say that?'

He stared. 'Can you imagine what it would have done to Simone?'

'It was Patty's baby!'

After a moment he said in a low voice. 'I don't know if she could have taken care of it.'

'Of course she could have!'

'She was very damaged.'

268

'Oh, for God's sake!'

He stared at his glass. 'It was just a mess,' he said, and now his voice was so low I could hardly hear. 'She wasn't well.'

'She was fine!'

'She took a torch to my car.'

'Is that all you care about?' I burst into tears. 'You didn't even ask about the baby!'

'Who's to say it was mine?'

In the silence I stared at the tissue in my hands.

'I'm sorry,' he said at last. 'What can I say? It was just – crazy. A kind of madness. And she was –' He shook his head.

'She was what?'

He let out a sigh. 'I hate myself for what I've done,' he said in a faint voice. 'For what I did to Simone. I'm not sure I can ever put it right.'

'She's still with you.'

'Yes.'

'And Patty's with Ed Kaplan.'

He pushed back his hair. 'Perhaps,' he said, 'it's for the best.'

'He tried to kill her!'

'I didn't mean –'

'He tried to *kill* her!'

The barman came over with a cloth. 'Same again?'

'No, thanks.'

It was two years before I saw Jean-Pierre again, and then it seemed like I had wandered into the wrong movie by mistake. It was a January night in New York; the wind so icy that my ears ached with pain. Clinton had become a hero, Hillary a senator – the dotcom madness had been and gone as if it had never existed.

I was outside the high windows of the Barnes and Noble on East 54th Street. Its neons cast shadows on the frozen banks of snow. Inside a muffled-up crowd attentively sipped glasses of wine. In front of them stood Simone. She had just published an award-winning book of photographs of men and women of the century – or so the bill-boards said.

The doors parted in a heated blast of air. Simone was answering questions. The years had been good to her: her face was fuller and somehow richer, her hair shorter and more curly. Though she wouldn't have worn that matronly red twin set when I knew her: she had liked hippyish clothes.

She sat down in a burst of clapping and I saw Jean-Pierre emerge from the crowd.

He looked different. He had grown a beard. His neck seemed shorter and he had a dissatisfied expression that had, I realised, always been there – a suggestion that things should, somehow, have gone better. He checked his watch and said some-thing to Simone. She smiled and shook her head. I thought there was something clear about her and something clouded about him – but that too, I realised, had always been the case.

Simone sat at a table to sign books. I pulled off

my hat and Jean-Pierre caught sight of me. He was standing by the biography section.

'My God,' he said. 'Lottie.'

I smiled. 'Hi.'

He seemed astonished. 'My God,' he said.

I smiled and for a moment we looked at each other, taking back the past. 'How are you?' I asked. He had lost, I thought, that indefinable magnetism he had always had: he looked like a mediocre middle-aged man with thin legs.

He folded his arms. 'I'm good. How are you?'

'Really good, thanks.'

'Are you living in New York?'

'No. Just over on a visit. For work.'

'An interview?'

'No. I don't do that any more. I was seeing a friend. Andrew Harrison. You might remember him, actually. From college.'

He shook his head.

'Anyway.' I shrugged.

He put his hands in his pockets. He was wearing a wedding ring I didn't remember having seen before.

'So are you still doing journalism?'

'Me?' He nodded. 'A desk job. Nothing very interesting.' He paused. 'Editing a section about property.'

We both looked over at Simone. She was talking to a tense Chinese woman in glasses.

'And you're married?' he asked.

'Married? No. I was engaged to be last year – but

271

it didn't work out. I'm seeing someone else, now. A photographer.'

'Well, great.' He smiled encouragingly. 'Great.'

Unhurriedly Simone handed the last book to a man with a moustache and yellow boots. She said something to the Chinese woman. Then she turned and saw me.

She stared as if at a vision – and leapt from her seat. 'My God! Where have you been?'

I smiled. 'Hi Simone.'

'My God! I can't believe it! Where did you go? I rang and rang!'

'You did?'

'But I told Jean: every day, every day. Anton said you'd gone to Africa.'

I shrugged. 'I did. I sold the house. I went away. I wanted a change.'

'But I was so worried! All I got was your message and it didn't say anything! Where did you go?'

'Kenya. Then Uganda.' I smiled. 'I finished the book.'

'You did?'

'But I put it away. It wasn't good enough.'

'Oh!'

'And now you're the published author!'

'Tsk.' She blew out her lips and met my eyes wryly. 'It's nothing. A lot of nonsense.'

We looked at each other.

'You're so different,' she said. 'I love your hair.'

'You're just the same.'

'Old. And fat.'

We laughed.

'So where are you living?' she said.

'In the country. A cottage in Sussex. It's lovely.'

'Is it?' She seemed to see enough in my eyes to reassure her, because she nodded with pleasure. 'We're in SoHo now. In a loft. Who'd have thought it?'

'And are you okay?'

'I'm okay,' she said, and I saw it was true. Her eyes were untroubled. 'We see Mark,' she said, 'often.'

Jean-Pierre came up. 'I'm afraid we have to go.'

'Not yet!'

Simone led me to the window. I smelled her spicy scent and the musty damp of her collar. 'Tell me,' she said. 'We heard you got married.'

'No. I got engaged last summer. But I called it off. It was for the best. I'm with someone else now. A photographer, actually.'

'He's kind?'

'Very.'

She bent over a picture. Her hand went over mine – rough, warm. 'I put her in the book,' she said, and she didn't need to say who. 'How is she? I think about her so often. She never knew how much I didn't hate her: how much I understood.'

My eyes pricked. 'I don't know.'

She shook her head. 'She was so radiant. I still wear the bracelet she gave me.'

'She was a child,' I said. 'I hope she's okay.'

'I do too.'

'And you?'

She gave me a look. 'We're happy. It was simple, after all: we both loved him, me and her. That's why I could understand.'

The Chinese woman came over. She had a man's walk and a cold handshake. 'We're all set.'

'Promise you'll call?' said Simone.

They went into the night, Jean-Pierre taking out a pack of cigarettes, the publicist barking into her phone. I watched them cross the snowy street and then they got into a cab and drove out of my life forever.

In the end I did find out what happened to Patty. Six months after I saw Jean-Pierre and Simone I came across a picture of her in *Hello!*. She was dancing with Ed Kaplan at some kind of ball. Her head was turned to the camera, and her smile was wide and apparently joyful.

I found the other picture a year later. She was in an advert for tampons in the American edition of *Good Housekeeping*. They had done some retouching, but it was definitely her.

Interviews with Kaplan referred to him first as single, then, in 2003, as living with his girlfriend Alina, a Polish model – they married in 2004. That was after he had been cleared of all charges and begun working for Arnold Schwarzenegger in LA.

I never heard from Patty.

Or so I thought.

Four years after she left I went to a drinks party in Notting Hill and bumped into the couple who had bought my old house. They sent me a stack of old post and on top of the pile was a letter from Patty. It was written in different-coloured pens on cheap blue notepaper headed 'Vee Bar Ranch, 2091 State Highway, 130 Laramie, Wyoming 82070'. There wasn't any date.

Dearest Lottie,

I had a dream last nite I was in a boat rushing down a tunnel and I managed to cling to a branch and escape and suddenly I was having a picnic with you in the park, like we used to. It made me remember everything and I thought Id write. I know you might not want to here from me and all. But maybe you wont mind when you were so kind to me when I got sick and we had some good times together.

How are you and did you meet Mr Right? I guess I didnt. Ed turned out to be kind of a cunt, I should have known that huh. Sorry I did'nt say good bye. He said he would marry me and we did have some fun but then he went off with another girl. It wasnt so bad, he used to get so mad, I never seemed to be what he wanted.

Im in Wyoming now. Its nice here and real quiet. I live with a sweet man called Frank. He lives out of town a way but he lets me use his truck and even though its quiet I am quite happy.

How is Mark David do you think he ever thinks of me. I wrote him once when I saw him on the TV but he didn't rite back. Its no surprise really I guess he was pretty mad. He was a real lovely guy though and they dont come along often. But I kind of knew hed never marry me. I expect hes with Christeen now. Im not the kind of girl men marry I dont think. A guy I met last year said I was a mistress not a wife and Frank says hes had a bellyful of marriage. But hes very kind. He collects cowboy stuff like old pistols and spurs and carves tables and chairs. And he's been good to me, my health hasnt been great, I have had troubles with my colon but I am still hear and thats the main thing!

Well I dont now if you are still talking to me but anyway I thought Id say hi and if you have any kids give them a kiss from me!

As for finding myself like we always talked about I think I am still looking but hope to get there soon!

From a loving Misfit and well meaning Friend

Patty B

I wrote back straightaway, a long letter. It came back 'Addressee Not Known'. I looked her up on Google – no trace. But when I had to go to Denver to research a biography that I was writing I decided to make the trip to Laramie. It was a

276

three-hour drive with the Snowy Mountains huddled like piles of white sugar, the prairie unrolling like a yellow rug.

The Vee Bar was a desolate place, the deserted guest cabins scattered amid trees, the air so thin that my skin seemed to desiccate by the second. When I finally tracked down a member of staff they hadn't heard of Patty. So I went into Centennial and asked at the diner. 'Oh, now, we used to have a real pretty girl here called Patsy,' said the waitress. She screwed up her face to remember. 'She went to work for Frankie at the old Byron place, isn't that right, Don? But he sold up. Couple of years ago now. Went to live with his daughter in Colorado.'

'See, you can't make no money on them ranches,' said Don. 'It's the same story all over. Just can't make 'em pay.'

'And I don't know what became of her,' the waitress said. 'Want to leave your number, case she calls by?'

I went into the street and drove down the road. After a mile I got out and stood staring at the prairie. It was bathed in clear light and the most profound silence I'd ever heard. I hoped she was standing somewhere in it too, struggling with her small powers and her diminishing hoard of hope.

ACKNOWLEDGEMENTS

With love and grateful thanks to Ben Faccini, Zoe Waldie, Koukla MacLehose, Hugo Rodger-Brown, Ravi Mirchandani, Dominique Rawley, Andrew Billen, William Chalmers, Andrew Harrison and Anthony Geadah.